Other Books by Harriet Steel

Becoming Lola

Salvation

City of Dreams

Following the Dream

The Inspector de Silva Mysteries:

Trouble in Nuala

Dark Clouds over Nuala

Offstage in Nuala

Short stories:

Dancing and other stories

AN INSPECTOR DE SILVA MYSTERY

FATAL FINDS
IN NUALA

HARRIET STEEL

First published 2018

Copyright © Harriet Steel

The author or authors assert their moral right under the Copyright, Designs and Patents Act, 1988, to be identified as the author or authors of this work. All Rights reserved. No part of this publication may be reproduced, copied, stored in a retrieval system, or transmitted, in any form or by any means, without the prior written consent of the copyright holder, nor be otherwise circulated in any form of binding or cover other than that in which it is published and without a similar condition being imposed on the subsequent purchaser.

MYS STEEL

Author's Note and Acknowledgements

Welcome to the fourth book in my Inspector de Silva mystery series. Like the earlier ones, this is a self-contained story but, wearing my reader's hat, I usually find that my enjoyment of a series is deepened by reading the books in order and getting to know major characters well. With that in mind, I have included thumbnail sketches of those featuring here who took a major part in previous stories. I have also reprinted this introduction, with apologies to those who have already read it.

Three years ago, I had the great good fortune to visit the island of Sri Lanka, the former Ceylon. I fell in love with the country straight away, awed by its tremendous natural beauty and the charm and friendliness of its people who seem to have recovered extraordinarily well from the tragic civil war between the two main ethnic groups, the Sinhalese and the Tamils. I had been planning to write a new detective series for some time and when I came home, I decided to set it in Ceylon in the 1930s, a time when British Colonial rule created interesting contrasts, and sometimes conflicts, with traditional culture. Thus, Inspector Shanti de Silva and his friends were born.

I owe many thanks to everyone who helped with this book. My editor, John Hudspith, was, as usual, invaluable and Jane Dixon Smith designed my favourite cover yet as well as the elegant layout. Praise from the many readers who told me that they enjoyed the three previous books in this series and wanted to know what Inspector de Silva and his friends got up to next encouraged me to keep going. Above all, heartfelt thanks go to my husband, Roger, without whose unfailing encouragement and support I might never have reached the end.

All characters in the book are fictitious with the exception of well-known historical figures. Nuala is also fictitious although loosely based on the town of Nuwara Eliya. Any mistakes are my own.

Characters who appear regularly in the Inspector de Silva Mysteries

Inspector Shanti de Silva. He began his police career in Ceylon's capital city, Colombo, but, in middle age, he married and accepted a promotion to inspector in charge of the small force in the hill town of Nuala. Likes: a quiet life with his beloved wife; his car; good food; his garden. Dislikes: interference in his work by his British masters; formal occasions. Race and religion: Sinhalese, Buddhist.

Sergeant Prasanna. In his mid-twenties, recently married, and doing well in his job. Likes: cricket and is exceptionally good at it. Race and religion: Sinhalese, Buddhist.

Constable Nadar. A few years younger than Prasanna and less confident. Married with a baby boy. Likes: his food; making toys for his baby son. Dislikes: sleepless nights. Race and religion: Tamil, Hindu.

The British:

Jane de Silva. She came to Ceylon as a governess to a wealthy colonial family and met and married de Silva a few years later. A no-nonsense lady with a dry sense of humour. Likes: detective novels, cinema, and dancing. Dislikes: snobbishness.

Archie Clutterbuck. Assistant government agent in Nuala and as such, responsible for administration and keeping law and order in the area. Likes: his Labrador, Darcy; fishing; hunting big game. Dislikes: being argued with; the heat.

Florence Clutterbuck. Archie's wife, a stout, forthright lady. Likes: being queen bee; organising other people. Dislikes: people who don't defer to her at all times.

William Petrie. Government agent for the Central Province and therefore Archie Clutterbuck's boss. A charming exterior hides a steely character. Likes: getting things done. Dislikes: inefficiency.

Lady Caroline Petrie. His wife and a titled lady in her own right. She is a charming and gentle person.

Doctor David Hebden. Doctor for the Nuala area. He travelled widely before ending up in Nuala. Unmarried and hitherto, under his professional shell, rather shy. Likes: cricket. Dislikes: formality.

CHAPTER 1

July 1937

As he peered through the Morris's rain-soaked windscreen, Inspector Shanti de Silva began to regret the impulse that had led him to arrange one of his occasional meetings with his counterpart in Hatton. Still, life couldn't stop just because it was the monsoon season. Inspector Singh at Hatton had treated him to an excellent lunch too. He might not admit that to Jane, in case she decided to put him on short rations at dinner.

Yet there was no getting away from the monsoon. The wipers were helpless to keep up with the torrential rain, and it was impossible to see more than twenty yards ahead. If he had to drive any slower, he might never get back to Nuala for dinner in any case. He resigned himself to the thought. It would be better for his waistline.

The car rounded a bend and he saw something blocking the road. Braking carefully to avoid skidding, he came to a halt. A roadworker hurried over to the car, his waterproof cape flapping in the wind. De Silva wound down the window.

'The road is closed, sahib,' the man said apologetically. 'A tree has come down.'

'How long to clear it?'

The roadworker waggled his head. 'Who knows, sahib?

It has only been reported a little time. I'm waiting for more men to come and help with the clearing. Tomorrow perhaps the road will be open again.'

It wasn't unreasonable, thought de Silva with a sigh. The tree couldn't have been down all that long; the road had been clear when he passed this way going to Hatton. Well, unless he wanted to return there, his only option was to go back to the last crossroads and take the old road to Nuala. From what he remembered of the state of its surface, he'd have to drive even more slowly than on this one, but at least he'd be able to sleep in his own bed tonight.

'I'll turn around,' he said to the roadworker. 'Good luck with your job. I hope you don't have to wait for too long for reinforcements.'

'Thank you, sahib.'

It took ten minutes to reach the crossroads. Piloting the Morris onto the old road, de Silva saw that his reservations hadn't been misplaced; the surface was pitted with numerous potholes. Some of them could probably swallow a rickshaw and would certainly do the Morris's axles no good at all if he went down one. Gingerly, he set off, weaving from one side of the road to the other in his efforts to avoid trouble. This kind of driving was anything but restful. Narrowly missing an enormous puddle in the depths of which lurked goodness knew what pitfalls; he made a mental note to postpone future visits to Hatton until the dry weather. It would have been no surprise if the wise carpenter of Benares had suddenly appeared, sailing along in his boat, or, as Jane's Christian religion had it, old Noah and his Ark.

Distracted by his musings about how all religions sought to explain cataclysmic weather in terms of a Divine plan, as well as by the need to concentrate on the road ahead, he didn't notice the change in the Morris's engine tone at first. But when he did, he realised with dismay that something was wrong. The engine spluttered again, and he felt a violent jolt. The Morris lost speed; a few yards later, it came to a complete halt.

Steam drifted over the bonnet. He wasn't sure whether it was the result of the fault, or simply the rain turning to vapour in the humid air. Whatever the case, he wasn't hopeful that he would be able to fix the problem out here. If he couldn't, it would be a job for Gopallawa Motors, and they were back in Nuala.

He reached over to the passenger seat and grabbed his raincoat and hat. Getting out of the car, he pulled them on and went to open the bonnet. He was no mechanic and his ideas were soon exhausted. For sure, this was a problem he'd need Gopallawa Motors to solve.

A glance at the sky told him that it would soon be dark. He had a choice: stay with the car and spend the night in the jungle or walk the rest of the way to town. He weighed up the options. If he walked fast, he might be on the outskirts in an hour or so. Maybe he would find a rickshaw man to take him home to Sunnybank. Alternatively, he could stay where he was and wait for another car to come by and rescue him, but then he might be waiting until morning. Dearly as he loved the Morris, she was not a comfortable bed.

It was an awkward job steering her to the side of the road on his own, but eventually he accomplished it. He made sure that the handbrake was firmly on and set off in the direction of town, head down into the wind.

Despite his waterproofs, he soon felt as soggy as yesterday's rice. On he trudged, mud splattering his trousers and rain dripping from the brim of his hat. It found its way through the tongues of his shoes and soaked his socks. His feet squelched at every step. Jane had counselled him against going down to Hatton today, and she had been right.

He reckoned he had walked about a mile when something that sounded very like a scream startled him; he stopped and listened. He wasn't afraid of it being a wild animal. They had too much sense to be on the prowl on a night like this, but something about the eerie cry unnerved him.

It came again, fading against the howl of the wind. He squared his shoulders. Perhaps he was imagining things and it *was* just the wind. Briskly, he stepped out once more.

Then his heart started to pound. A pinpoint of white light was emerging from the darkness, dipping and swaying, emitting an inhuman wail.

He didn't think of himself as a superstitious man, but all reason deserted him. The Mohini! It must be the Mohini of ancient legend. The weeping, spirit-woman who haunted lonely roads, her dead baby in her arms. She begged her victims to help her, but if they did…

His blood froze as he remembered the old tales.

She was nearly on him! Her light dazzled him. Sweat poured from his forehead, mingling with the rain. His vision blurring, his breath came in ragged gasps. The ground caught at his feet like glue. In a burst of desperation, he wrenched himself free and ran, blundering into puddles and potholes; stumbling over the debris the storm had tossed onto the road. The cries grew louder.

Then something struck him, and there was darkness.

CHAPTER 2

'Lucky for you that young Frobisher was also coming home from Hatton last night,' said Archie Clutterbuck. 'He was down there for me on official business. Even luckier he didn't run you over. He told me he saw you in the nick of time and just managed to stop. If it hadn't been for that branch coming down and hitting you on the head, there would have been no harm done.'

De Silva swallowed. He had no intention of admitting his foolishness to his boss, the assistant government agent. Far from being the ghastly apparition he had feared, the white light had heralded the approach of Charlie Frobisher, a new member of the Residence's staff. One of Frobisher's car's headlights had been out, and the heavy rain had done the rest. As far as Frobisher was concerned, de Silva hadn't been running as if his life depended on it; he had simply been the victim of a freak accident, knocked out by a dead branch brought down by the high wind.

'I'm most grateful to him. Would you convey my thanks? I don't know how I would have got home without his help.'

'No lasting ill effects, I hope?'

'Only a slight headache.'

'Good; but you obviously took quite a knock from that branch. You must speak to Doctor Hebden if the headache gets any worse. I'm sure Mrs de Silva would say the same.'

Jane would, and indeed she had in no uncertain terms.

'Damnable time of year,' Clutterbuck went on, conversationally. 'Haven't had a game of golf in weeks. Course is completely waterlogged, or so the head greenkeeper tells me. No shooting and precious little fishing to be done either.'

He glanced at the elderly Labrador snoozing in front of the cheerful fire.

'Just as well old Darcy doesn't need as much exercise as he did when he was a youngster. I think he'd toast himself in front of that fire all day if I didn't push him out occasionally.'

From the pungent smell of drying dog, de Silva guessed that there had been a recent sortie.

'Well, apart from running around in the dark getting yourself into scrapes, have you anything to report?'

'Nothing of any importance, sir. My visit to Hatton was merely a routine one. I like to keep up with Inspector Singh down there.'

'Good plan. Never know when you might need his cooperation, and then personal acquaintance is invaluable. It's not what you know, it's who you know, eh?'

'Quite right, sir.'

Clutterbuck looked at his wristwatch. 'I have a luncheon appointment in an hour, but I hope you'll take a pre-prandial with me before you go. Something to keep out the damp, eh?'

De Silva smiled. 'Exactly, sir.'

'Whisky and soda?'

'That would be most welcome.'

* * *

Twenty minutes later, fortified by a considerably stronger whisky and soda than he would have poured for himself, de Silva emerged onto the rainswept drive and hurried over to the car Gopallawa Motors had lent him while the Morris was out of action.

As he drove back to the station, he thought again about the incident on the road. He still wasn't completely convinced that there was nothing more to it than Charlie Frobisher driving towards him and then the disastrous encounter with the falling branch. When he'd told Jane she had, of course, dismissed any other possibilities.

'Those screams you thought you heard were the wind, dear,' she'd said firmly. 'And if both of Charlie Frobisher's headlights had been working, I'm sure you would have realised, even at a distance, that it was a car coming towards you.'

He sneezed and took a hand from the steering wheel to reach in his pocket for his handkerchief. The belief in the stars and the spirit world that he had grown up with was sometimes hard to shake off — he hoped this cold wasn't going to be equally intractable — but of course Jane was right.

He'd woken that morning with a very scratchy throat and a feverish feeling. Jane had tried to persuade him to take the day off, but he hadn't wanted to miss his regular appointment with Clutterbuck. There were also arrangements to be made for recovering the Morris. He had already spoken to the manager at Gopallawa Motors and would be spending the afternoon going out with two of the garage's mechanics to see what could be done. If the Morris couldn't be fixed by the roadside, they would have to tow her back and deal with the problem in town. He hoped that wouldn't take long. The car that Gopallawa had lent him was adequate for a day or two, but it was no substitute.

Another sneeze shook him, and he blew his nose once

more. In the rear-view mirror, he noticed his eyes were already rimmed with pink. He grimaced; it looked like he wasn't going to be able to avoid this cold.

CHAPTER 3

At the police station, he was surprised to find Sergeant Prasanna's wife, Kuveni, sitting with her husband and Constable Nadar in the public room. He and Jane had become very fond of Kuveni when she lived with them for a few months before her marriage, and he was always delighted to see her, but she rarely came to the station. All three of them stood up as he entered, but he motioned Kuveni to sit down again.

'No need to get up for me, my dear. You're well, I trust? It can't be long until the baby's due. I hope your rascal of a husband is taking great care of you.'

'Oh, he is, Inspector.' Kuveni gave him a smile that accentuated the dimples in her cheeks. 'He is very helpful in the house.'

'Excellent. Now, I'm delighted to see you but also anxious to be reassured that your visit is not due to some problem.'

There was a movement in the corner of the room and for the first time, he noticed there was a small, thin woman huddled there, watching him with frightened eyes. From the look of her clothes, she wasn't well off. Her face was careworn.

'Who is this?' he asked.

The woman's hands twisted a fold of her sari; she glanced anxiously at Kuveni who spoke to her in the Vedda language. The woman was silent for a moment then made a halting reply. Even though de Silva spoke English, Tamil and Sinhalese, he had never learnt the ancient tongue of the Veddas, a dwindling race that most Ceylonese considered primitive, although Kuveni was living proof that with education and opportunity, they could hold their own against Ceylon's other inhabitants.

'Does she only speak Vedda?' he asked.

Kuveni shook her head. 'She speaks some Tamil, Inspector, but she is afraid. She is not used to coming to a place like this.'

'I see.'

He went over to the woman and took her hand. 'There's no need to be frightened,' he said gently in Tamil. 'I'm here to help you.'

The woman must have understood him for a shy smile softened her face. 'Thank you,' she whispered.

With prompting from Kuveni where her Tamil failed her, the woman explained that her husband, Velu, was missing.

'How many days has he been gone?' asked de Silva.

'Two days before last poya day.'

De Silva scratched his chin. Poya day was the day of the full moon; the last one had fallen a week ago. He knew that Vedda men liked to go on hunting trips into the jungle, often, unfortunately, without the requisite government licence, but an absence of eight or nine days did seem unusual, particularly if the man had a wife.

'Where do you live?'

The woman glanced at Kuveni who spoke for her. 'Her home is in the village where I lived with my father and my brother, Vijay, before I came to Nuala.'

'Close to the old Hatton road then.'

'Yes. At least, she and her husband live on the fringe of the village. The headman and the other villagers do not welcome them.'

De Silva remembered Kuveni's own difficulties in her old village. Her family too had been forced to live on the outskirts of the village. He was glad that marriage to Prasanna had enabled her to put all that behind her.

'How well do you know her, Kuveni? She looks much older than you.'

'Quite well, although we are different ages.' She gave de Silva an anxious look. 'My brother sometimes worked with her husband as a tracker for hunters.'

Hmm, probably an irregular activity, thought de Silva. Tracking jobs were lucrative and much sought after. Local men who were well versed in the geography of their area and skilled at finding game for hunters could expect generous tips as well as good daily pay. To avoid jealousies and problems, as well as making money for the British, tracking jobs were tightly controlled by a system of government licences and habitually given to Sinhalese or Tamils. Still, he wasn't going to make an issue of that today.

'She told me she wanted to better herself,' Kuveni continued. 'For several months she has been walking into town to see if I have any work for her. If I can, I employ her to do simple sewing.'

De Silva nodded. He knew that the beautiful saris Kuveni made in her business required considerable skill in embroidery, but there was clearly some plain sewing to be done too.

'So, she came to you for help with this matter of her missing husband?'

'Yes.'

'And does she have children to provide for?'

The woman understood and shook her head.

'Perhaps in the circumstances that's a blessing.'

'With your permission, sir,' Prasanna cut in, 'Nadar and I would like to spend some time searching the area for her husband.'

De Silva hesitated. Was this really a good use of police time? It was a vast area.

Then a memory stirred: that sound he had heard in the storm. Jane was probably right that it was the wind but what if…? They could at least search in the area close to where the Morris had broken down.

He nodded to Prasanna. 'Very well. There's nothing much for you to do here today, so you may as well go there this afternoon and have a look round. In fact, I'll be driving in that direction. My car broke down last night on the old Hatton road. I'm meeting some of Gopallawa's men there to see what needs to be done. You can join me. It's somewhere to make a start, I suppose.'

He glanced at the woman. 'Have you understood what we've been saying?'

Shyly, she shook her head then brightened a little as Kuveni explained.

'Have you or Nadar ever seen this man, Velu?' de Silva asked Prasanna.

'No, sir, but the lady has described him to us.'

'Good. I think that's all we can do for now.'

He smiled at Kuveni. 'It's a great pleasure to see you, my dear. Jane will be very glad to hear you're well.'

Prasanna ushered the two women out. When he returned, he looked gloomy.

'What's wrong?' asked de Silva.

'Thank you for agreeing to a search, sir, but I think it will be very hard to find this Velu. I only asked to please Kuveni. The jungle stretches for miles, and he may not even want to be found.'

'You mean he might want to leave his wife?' asked Nadar, frowning.

'Perhaps. Or he may have been killed and eaten by an animal.'

'We can't discount the possibility,' said de Silva.

He looked at their downcast faces and wondered whether to mention the scream he thought he'd heard, then decided not to. He'd rather keep the panic he felt that night to himself. In any case, it would be a remarkable coincidence if the scream had come from this man Velu at just the moment he, de Silva, had been in the vicinity to hear it.

'Cheer up,' he said briskly. 'We've told the woman we'll search and search we will.'

He crossed to the door of his office and opened it. 'I have some paperwork to do. Bring me a cup of tea and then fetch me my usual lunch from the place near the post office. It will be quicker than going home and we'll set off once I've eaten. Oh, and one of you telephone Gopallawa. Tell him we'll probably leave here in an hour or so.'

'Yes, sir,' the young men chorused.

A few minutes later, Nadar brought in the tea and shortly afterwards, Prasanna came back with a miniature feast: two kinds of vegetable curry, a large serving of fragrant rice and a crisp round of well-charred naan bread glistening with ghee.

As de Silva ate, he thought about the missing villager and his unhappy wife. If she had been abandoned, he felt very sorry for her. Life was hard enough for Vedda people without having a personal betrayal to bear. He wondered what was behind it. Had the husband found a younger woman whom he preferred? Kuveni said the woman had no children; that might have caused problems between the couple too. As villagers grew older, they relied on children to support them. A childless couple faced more than the normal hardships.

He finished his lunch and decided to close his eyes for a while. Jane liked to tease him about his fondness for regular naps, but he doubted that another twenty minutes or so would make any difference. Sadly, the hard truth was that it was extremely unlikely that this unfortunate woman's story would have a happy ending.

CHAPTER 4

The mechanics from Gopallawa Motors were already with the Morris by the time de Silva arrived with Prasanna and Nadar. The elder mechanic hurried over.

'We have found the problem, sahib.'

De Silva listened to the lengthy explanation.

'We can make a temporary repair,' the mechanic finished, 'but the car will need to come to the garage for more work before it is reliable to drive again. And it will be best if I drive it there in case of more difficulties on the way.'

Reluctantly, de Silva nodded. Even though he recognised the mechanic and knew that he had worked for Gopallawa for many years, it went against the grain to hand his beloved Morris over to another driver.

'How long is the repair likely to take?'

'Perhaps a week, sahib. We may have to order a new part from Kandy.'

De Silva sighed. He had been hoping that the trouble and expense would be minimal; it seemed he was to be disappointed.

'I see. Well, tell your boss I'll keep this car until mine's ready. He may add something to the bill, but not too much, mind.'

The man grinned. 'I will tell him, sahib.'

'I'll leave you to get on with the job.'

'Thank you, sahib.'

The mechanic walked back to the Morris.

'Shall we begin the search now, sir?' asked Prasanna.

'You may as well.'

The three of them stared at the near-impenetrable walls of green flanking either side of the road. Glancing at Prasanna and Nadar, de Silva saw that, now they were about to embark on it, they were totally daunted by the scale of the task they had taken on. If this villager, Velu, had chosen to disappear, the search would be a waste of time anyway; he was probably long gone by now. Perhaps it would be wise to call it off. But then he thought of Kuveni and the man's wife. He didn't want to let them down. Anyway, it was still too early to rule out the possibility that the man had fallen victim to a wild animal. Even the cleverest of trackers made mistakes that cost them their lives.

'How close is the village to where we are now?'

'Quite close, sir,' answered Prasanna.

'Right; I'll give you a bit of help to start off with. It can do no harm to drive very slowly back towards Nuala and look out for anything unusual. You two keep watch. If you see anything out of the ordinary, shout out, and we can stop and investigate.'

'What kind of thing do you mean, sir?' asked Nadar.

'I don't know until I see it. Just keep your eyes wide open. If we find nothing, it might be best to call off the search, but I'll make that decision when the time comes.'

'Yes, sir,' said Prasanna. He looked relieved.

They climbed into the car. De Silva started the engine and set off at a snail's pace. At first, they saw nothing untoward apart from a giant monitor lizard basking on the hot tarmac. It moved sluggishly into the undergrowth at their stately approach.

De Silva was beginning to think that the exercise was a waste of time when Nadar shouted from the back seat. De Silva drew to a halt and swivelled round. 'What have you seen?'

'It looks like there's a track leading into the trees, sir.'

'Right; let's take a look.'

The three men got out and walked back to the place Nadar indicated. The break in the trees was narrow but it certainly seemed that someone, or something, had passed that way recently, either entering or leaving the jungle. Even through his cold, the smell of damp earth and leaf mould invaded de Silva's nostrils. Prasanna inched in then crouched down and studied the ground.

'No sign of footprints, sir. Although if a man was light and used to moving stealthily, he might not leave any tracks in this leaf mould.'

'I suppose that's true, but it doesn't help us much. Go a bit further in.'

Prasanna straightened up and took a few more paces into the trees then crouched down again. He picked up a stick and flicked some of the leaf mould aside. 'Animal droppings, sir.'

'A predator?'

Prasanna shook his head. 'From the look of them, sir, my guess is they were left by a deer.'

'Pity, I thought we might have something. Never mind, we'll carry on.'

Back in the car, their crawling progress resumed. A little further on, a glint to the right-hand side of the road caught de Silva's eye. Suddenly, he remembered that on his night walk, before the white light spooked him, he'd noticed a stream coming in from the trees and running under the road. Last night, thanks to the monsoon rain, it had been a torrent, but already the water level had gone down, and it flowed sluggishly through a jumble of boulders, fallen timber and jungle detritus. He wondered if, in its present state, it might provide a pathway through the trees. Could the missing villager, Velu, have come this way? Had he been surprised by an animal at some point?

'Shall we follow it for a little way, sir?' asked Prasanna.

On brief reflection, de Silva had his doubts the stream would reveal anything useful, but it could do no harm checking. He nodded. 'But don't spend too long. I'll wait with the car.'

He leant against the bonnet as the two young men picked their way over the stones in the stream's bed, clutching at overhanging branches when their balance faltered. After a few moments, they disappeared. Their voices faded, to be replaced by the sounds of the jungle: the burble of the stream; the whistle of unseen birds high up in the tree canopy, and the hum of millions of insects.

All at once, de Silva felt a wave of apprehension come over him. He would normally be untroubled. Perhaps the villager's mysterious disappearance, added to the unnerving experience of the previous night, made him ill at ease. The green walls of the jungle seemed menacing, and a shiver went through him as his imagination conjured up visions of blood-hungry demons with fiery eyes and fangs dripping gore, lying in wait for solitary travellers like himself.

'Sir! Sir!'

The voice wrenched him back to a very welcome reality. He recovered his composure and saw Prasanna jumping from a stone back onto the road, kicking up a spray of water behind him.

'We've found something, sir!'

'What?'

'It looks like someone was digging a hole back there.' He indicated with his thumb over his right shoulder. 'It's quite a way in but I think you should come and see, sir. I've left Nadar digging, but it would help if we had better tools than the stick he's using.'

'Look in the car boot. You might find something there.'

A quick search revealed a shovel with a long handle. It was the type of implement many people carried in the monsoon season in case they needed to scrape away thick mud that had washed onto the road, or, in the worst case, dig out a vehicle that had skidded off the road into a ditch.

Shouldering it, Prasanna headed back along the stream. De Silva followed cautiously, testing the stones before he put his weight on them, wary of their coatings of slimy moss, but after a few minutes, he became more confident and managed to keep up. It was a while since he'd done anything more strenuous than tend his roses, so it was good to know he hadn't completely lost his touch. In the Colombo days of his youth, he'd had plenty of stamina and been able to muster a perfectly creditable turn of speed. Frequently, he'd needed it when he was pursuing a criminal.

By the time he reached the place where Nadar was scraping away at the earth, however, he was starting to feel out of puff. Prasanna handed Nadar the shovel. The patch of disturbed ground that lay before them was about six feet long by three feet wide. It must have been dug over not many days ago for, despite the speed of growth in the jungle, the vegetation hadn't had time to inch back.

Nadar started to dig again, but, in the humid heat, he was soon dripping. Prasanna took over and de Silva watched with mounting interest. Whoever had excavated this hole before them had sliced so cleanly through the network of roots that marbled the soil that they must have used a sharp implement. No animal would dig in such a way.

Even through his cold, de Silva became aware of a nauseating smell: a smell that was horribly familiar. His stomach roiled.

Prasanna stopped digging and rested the shovel against a nearby tree. He hunkered down and picked up a flat stone that lay nearby, then began to tease the earth away from an object that was half-buried in the soil. After a few scrapes, he recoiled. His face turned pale and sweat beaded his forehead.

'This isn't a root, sir.'

'You'd better let me carry on,' de Silva said quietly. 'Stand back if you want. I'm afraid this isn't going to be a pretty sight.'

Taking the stone from Prasanna, he crouched by the hole and worked the soil away from the buried object. Gradually, the contour of an arm appeared, then a shoulder. Moving up, the soil was dark; de Silva knew it was stained with blood. Steeling himself, he continued with his grisly task.

Revealed at last, the man lay on his back, flung unceremoniously into his makeshift grave. His filthy hair, matted with blood, fanned out around a face so badly damaged as to be unrecognisable. Blood caked his upper body. He had been shot in the head and in the region of the heart. His killer hadn't left anything to chance. By the look of him, thought de Silva, he's been dead for several days, so it's impossible that the noises I heard were his dying cries. Perhaps though, some supernatural power took a hand in causing the Morris to break down close by the right place.

He frowned and banished the thought. He mustn't let superstitious fears take control. He'd made enough of a fool of himself over the Mohini. Hearing hurrying feet behind him, he glanced over his shoulder to find that Nadar was in the bushes. The sound of retching followed. Poor lad, it was probably the first time he'd had to face a sight like this one. It was good to see that Prasanna was coping. De Silva motioned him to come closer.

'Do you think he's our man?'

Prasanna pointed to the livid scar running diagonally across the dead man's right shoulder. 'I think he might be, sir. It's impossible to tell from his face, I know, but his wife mentioned he had a scar like that one.'

He looked at the man's hands. 'She said he was missing the fourth finger on his right hand too, just as this man is.'

De Silva sighed. 'The evidence seems sufficiently

conclusive. Poor woman: although I imagine she already fears the worst. I wonder how much she knew about her husband's activities. This clearly isn't a case of falling victim to an animal. We'll need to question her again, I'm afraid. I'd better get back to Nuala and arrange to have the body brought in. Whatever he did, the fellow ought to have a decent burial. The two of you had better stay until the undertakers come. I don't want to cover the body up again and now it will be a magnet for predators.'

He removed his uniform jacket, unbuckled the holster containing his Webley and handed it to Prasanna. 'Here, you'd better keep this with you. You might need to defend yourselves.'

'Thank you, sir.'

'I'll be back as soon as I can.'

* * *

When he reached the police station, de Silva telephoned the undertakers in Hatton. Fortunately, they were able to send the black station wagon they used as a hearse straight away. De Silva drove back to the old Hatton road to find Prasanna on his own.

'Where's Nadar got to?'

'He's having a look round, sir.'

'Oh? Why's that?'

'He noticed something glinting in the stream when he went to wash off the shovel. It was a coin, in fact there were several. He's gone back to see if he can find anything else.'

'Coins? That seems odd. Do you have them here?'

'Yes, sir.'

Prasanna fished in one of his pockets and produced some tarnished coins, each about the size of his thumbnail.

De Silva took them and studied them. Whatever was

marked on them was too worn away to make out, but they looked quite old. 'They may not have any connection with this fellow, but it's a strange place to find them. Have you checked his trouser pockets?'

'No, sir. We didn't like to disturb anything without your permission.'

'Very laudable.'

De Silva glanced dubiously at the body. He didn't fancy getting close to it again himself, but it was necessary. He pulled out a handkerchief and held it over his nose and mouth. With luck, that would make the operation more bearable.

There was nothing in the pockets of the dead man's ragged trousers but, remembering an old trick thieves liked to pull in his Colombo days, de Silva unrolled the turned-up hems. The first turn-up was empty, but two more coins fell out of the other one.

He straightened and took a few steps back before removing the handkerchief from his face. 'It seems there is a connection. I wonder how he came by these.'

Nadar emerged from the trees.

'Any luck?' asked de Silva. 'Prasanna and I have just found more coins in the deceased's clothing.'

Nadar held out some small pieces of metal that looked like gold. 'They were in the bed of the stream near the coins, sir. I didn't notice them at first.'

De Silva took the pieces. They were decoratively worked and apparently part of some larger object or objects.

'Hmm, they may be from jewellery of some kind: brooches or hair ornaments. Interesting; our man might have been trying to make off with these and the coins then dropped them when he was attacked. What I'd really like to know is how he got them. We'll take them along with us once the undertakers have dealt with the body.'

CHAPTER 5

There was only a little daylight left by the time the undertakers drove away with their grim cargo. De Silva had already decided to spare Kuveni's friend the distress of a formal identification. He was sure in his own mind that the dead man was her husband, Velu.

He returned to the police station with Prasanna and Nadar and, with their help, wrote up a report of the afternoon's work.

'You may as well get off home now,' he said when they had finished. 'I'll see Mr Clutterbuck in the morning and then decide where we go from here. Do you have any idea where Velu's widow is now?'

'I expect she'll be at my house with Kuveni, sir,' said Prasanna. 'Kuveni didn't want to send her back to the village without knowing where her husband was. A neighbour there promised to send a message if he returned in the meantime.'

'Are you prepared to break the news to her?'

Prasanna nodded. 'Yes, sir. I'm sure Kuveni will help me. We'll tell her as kindly as possible.'

'Good; there's no need to give her too many details.'

'I understand, sir.'

'Well, if I go straight to the Residence tomorrow, I doubt I'll be back here much before midday. It will do no harm for the station to be closed for a couple of hours. I'd like the two of you to go to the bazaar. See if anyone's selling coins or jewellery matching what we found today.'

'Shall we take what we have with us, sir?' asked Nadar. 'One of the stallholders might recognise something.'

'Not for the moment: I don't want to arouse suspicion. Look round the stalls but keep quiet about what you're looking for. If there are any questions, drop a hint or two about contraband cigarettes or alcohol.'

He pulled out his handkerchief and blew his nose. This wretched cold was getting worse. He wanted to be home, preferably with a stiff whisky in his hand. 'Goodnight, both of you. Do your best tomorrow.'

* * *

'Oh dear, your cold sounds dreadful this evening,' said Jane.

De Silva poured two fingers of whisky into a glass and topped up with soda from the syphon. 'I have a head full of lamb's wool,' he said gloomily.

'Cotton wool, dear.'

'Whatever kind of wool it is, it's most unpleasant. Will you have a sherry to keep me company?'

'Thank you, a small one would be nice.'

He poured a sherry and brought it over to her then settled down in his armchair, cradling his glass of whisky in his hands.

'I feel so sorry for this poor woman,' said Jane. 'Not only has she lost her husband, but you say he died in such a brutal way. I do hope Prasanna will be careful how much he tells her.'

'I've told him to spare her the details.'

'We ought to do something for her.'

'What do you have in mind?'

'Perhaps we could raise some money to make her life a

little easier.' She took a sip of sherry. 'It's a blessing there are no children.'

He shrugged. 'Although most villagers see children as an insurance for their old age; that is, if they live long enough to have one.'

'Do you have any idea who might have wanted this man, Velu, dead?'

'Not yet, but he had a few interesting items on him, and Nadar discovered more in the stream we walked along before we found the grave. I've brought them home to show you.'

He went out to the hall and fetched the box in which he'd stowed the coins and pieces of metal. He put it in Jane's lap.

She lifted the lid and picked up one of the coins then held it to the light. 'How thin the metal is. Do you think these are very old?'

'I've no idea, but it would be good to find someone who can tell me if they're valuable.'

Replacing the coin in the box, Jane took out the metal pieces and studied them. 'The patterns on them are very pretty,' she said at last.

'I thought they might be parts of brooches or hair ornaments. Something like that anyway.'

'That's possible. Are they made of gold, do you think?'

'I'm not sure, but they look like it, and I definitely need to find out more.'

He pulled out his handkerchief, blew his nose and mopped his eyes. 'In fact, it's imperative that I do. Apart from the coins and these pieces, I don't have a single lead.'

'Do you think this man Velu stole them?'

'I doubt he acquired them legally. A man like him would be extremely unlikely to have the money to buy jewellery. As for the coins, they're not the currency we use today, so there would be no practical reason why he had them. If they were current, I might have assumed they were tips he received from game hunters.'

'Are you certain that he was a tracker?'

'Yes; Kuveni told me he worked with her brother sometimes. That's how she came to know his widow.' He drained his whisky. 'Have I time for another small one before dinner?'

'If you like, dear.'

He grinned. 'Do I detect a hint of disapproval? It's purely for medicinal purposes, I assure you.'

Jane laughed. 'I'm sure it is, dear; you have got a very nasty cold. Why not have an early night after we've eaten?'

'I think I will.'

Glancing out of the window, he saw that the wind was lashing the trees and flinging great handfuls of rain across the lawn. His beloved garden would be a sea of mud by morning. 'I certainly won't be taking an evening walk in this. The last thing I need is another soaking.'

He yawned. 'I'll go and see Archie Clutterbuck first thing in the morning. He doesn't know about the case yet. I thought it was better to wait. Catching him at the end of the day's not always a wise move. I want him in a good mood, or he might think the death of a villager not all that important.'

Jane frowned. 'Even when it's clearly murder? That would be disgraceful.'

'It would, and he's a decent man at heart. Nevertheless, it's always advisable to handle him in the right way.'

CHAPTER 6

The following morning, de Silva telephoned the Residence to find that Archie Clutterbuck was in meetings until midday but would see him then. He decided to spend the intervening time at home and allow himself some rest. He had moved to one of the bungalow's spare rooms to avoid disturbing Jane with his cold and had passed a restless night. Contemplating the prospect of the conversation with his boss, he hoped Clutterbuck wasn't going to be in one of his irritable moods.

'It's bad enough having a thick head,' he remarked to Jane as he ate a late breakfast. 'Let alone having to deal with Archie. Especially as monsoon weather tends to make him fidgety.'

'Understandable, I suppose. People like him are happiest out of doors.'

'Hmm.'

He glanced out of the window. He had lain awake listening to the rain on the bungalow's roof for much of the night, but it seemed that the clouds still hadn't exhausted their supply of water. On the drive to the Residence, he took the precaution of driving more slowly than usual.

A servant showed him into Clutterbuck's study where he found the assistant government agent – golf club in hand – practising his putting into the narrow space between two paperweights set down on a Persian rug. He looked up and nodded at de Silva. 'This dratted rain; have to keep in practise somehow. Don't tell Mrs Clutterbuck. She thinks I'm hard at work.'

That was a relief, thought de Silva. Archie was in one of his jovial moods. It was safe to anticipate he would be cooperative.

'A bad business,' he said grimly when de Silva had explained the situation. 'Where's the body now?'

'The undertakers have taken it to the mortuary at Hatton.'

'Not much point arranging a post-mortem; the cause of death seems abundantly clear.'

'I agree, sir.'

'Has the widow been informed?'

'I expect she has been by now. Sergeant Prasanna and his wife took on that unpleasant duty.'

'Then I suggest you release the body to her as soon as possible. If she has no family to help her, I'll instruct my office to provide funds for the funeral.'

'That's good of you, sir.'

'Least one can do under the circumstances. Any idea who might be responsible for the murder?'

'Not yet, sir.'

'I imagine a private feud of some kind is probably behind it. Have you been to the village yet?'

De Silva sneezed. 'No, but I intend to, of course.'

'Why not send one of your men? You don't look too fit to me, and it will be good experience for them.'

'I might do that, sir.'

It was true it would be good for Prasanna and Nadar to take more responsibility, and the villagers might talk more readily to someone less senior. He could always pay a second visit later if it seemed necessary.

'I'll ask around my staff and see if anyone has personal experience of the headman,' Clutterbuck went on. 'Always handy to know more about the people you're dealing with than they do about you.'

'Thank you, sir.'

Clutterbuck's eyes slid to the golf club leaning against his desk.

'There is one more thing, sir,' said de Silva.

'Yes?'

As de Silva described what they'd found near Velu's body, he sensed that Clutterbuck wasn't particularly interested, but he ploughed on.

'Have you brought any of these pieces with you?' asked Clutterbuck when he finished. There was a note of impatience in his voice.

De Silva opened the box he had brought with him, unrolled the cloth in which he'd wrapped the coins and metal pieces and put them on Clutterbuck's desk.

Clutterbuck inspected the haul for a few moments. 'Not my line of country,' he said with a shrug.

'With your permission, sir, I'd like to find out more about them.'

His boss rubbed the bridge of his nose and pondered for a few moments. 'You have a point, but I've no idea who could help us up here, and I'm in two minds whether it's worth making a trip to Colombo or even Kandy.'

'I think it might be, sir.'

There was a longer pause. 'I remember now,' Clutterbuck said at last. 'There is a fellow who might be able to throw a bit of light on the matter; his name's Henry Coryat. He's a bit of a hermit these days, but I believe he was very eminent in his field when he worked at the museum down in Colombo. Mrs Clutterbuck tried to involve him in the social whirl when he first arrived in Nuala. If memory serves, he played a decent hand of bridge, although he wasn't much use for anything else. But he soon made it clear he preferred to be left alone. Lives in a bungalow way out of town. I think he has a telephone though, and the telephonist should still have the number. If so, I'll contact him and ask if he'll see you.'

'Thank you, sir.'

Clutterbuck looked at the clock on the mantelpiece. 'No time like the present. If he's willing, shall I suggest you motor out after lunch?'

The telephonist did indeed have the number and the call didn't take long. Obviously, Henry Coryat was a man of few words. Clutterbuck replaced the receiver. 'That's done. He's expecting you this afternoon. Come back and let me know how you got on, will you? I'll be here all day tomorrow.'

'I will, sir.'

* * *

'I'm glad it went well, dear,' said Jane as they ate lunch at Sunnybank. 'But please drive carefully to Mr Coryat's house. That area's very deserted; the road's bound to be rough.'

'Don't worry, I'll be careful.'

'I met Henry Coryat once or twice at the Clutterbucks,' Jane mused. 'Absolutely no small talk, although I'm sure he's very interesting on his subject.'

'I don't need to know his views on the cricket, or the latest cinema release.'

Jane looked at him sympathetically. 'Are you still feeling poorly?'

'Does it show?'

'A little. Why not take Archie's advice and send Prasanna and Nadar out to the village to talk to the headman?'

'I might just do that.'

He sighed. 'But I ought to visit this fellow Henry Coryat myself. Being British, I doubt he'd take kindly to being interviewed by my subordinates.'

'I expect you're right. What a nuisance for you, but perhaps something useful will come of it.'

'Let's hope so.'

* * *

The road to Henry Coryat's house was as rough as Jane had predicted. In places, it snaked along the flanks of hillsides, rising in a series of hairpin bends that de Silva negotiated very cautiously. He was relieved when the road levelled out and ran in a more-or-less straight line between plantations of rubber and banana trees.

Freed from the necessity of concentrating solely on his driving, he turned his mind to the prospect of the interview with Coryat. From what Archie said, he wasn't going to be the easiest of men to deal with, but he had agreed to meet. That was reasonably encouraging.

There was a gap in the trees to the left of the road, and he caught his first glimpse of the bungalow. It was built close to the edge of a plateau. Where it ended, the land fell steeply away once more. The bungalow must enjoy magnificent views to make up for its isolated situation.

Fifty yards further on, de Silva reached some gates. Fortunately, they were open, so he drove through and into the bungalow's grounds. It was clear that Coryat's interests didn't lie in the direction of gardening. The drive ran between tangles of overgrown shrubs, and after that, an unkempt lawn, dotted with a few bushes and weedy flower-beds lay between him and the bungalow. Roses struggled to lift their heads above the weeds. De Silva recognised some of the varieties; they were sturdy favourites, and his fingers itched to rescue them.

He parked and went up to the front door. The paintwork on it and the window frames was dry and flaking. De Silva guessed that the glass hadn't been cleaned for many months. A dark green stain ran down one wall; above it jutted the cause: a broken section of guttering.

There was no sign of life, and when he rang the doorbell, it was a long time before he heard the rattle of a chain being undone. The door opened, and an elderly man stood on the threshold. He was pale, with sparse, grey hair and a long, untrimmed beard. A tweed jacket and cavalry twills that had both seen better days hung on him as if they had been made for a much larger man. Watery blue eyes with heavy pouches under the lower lids regarded de Silva sceptically.

'I presume you're the policeman.'

'I am, sir.'

De Silva was surprised that Coryat had answered the door himself but was careful not to show it.

'You'd better come in.'

'Thank you; it's very good of you to see me at such short notice.'

Coryat grunted by way of acknowledgment. 'We'll talk in my study.'

De Silva followed him down a dimly lit passageway that led to a gloomy room. The walls were lined with glass-fronted bookcases; presumably, they ensured that Coryat's extensive library remained free of dust, which certainly wasn't the case with the rest of the contents of the room. He noticed the washed-out red curtains hanging at the windows and the uninviting armchairs on either side of the fireplace. On the wall above, there was a flyblown watercolour in an ugly frame: the only picture in the room. It showed antique ruins that dwarfed the sketchily depicted figures standing among their stone columns and crumbling walls. The place looked vaguely familiar.

'Anuradhapura,' said Coryat. 'When I first came to Ceylon, I spent several years on the excavations there.'

Of course, the ancient city to the north of Kandy. Centuries ago, it had been Ceylon's capital.

'When was that, sir?'

'Before the war.' An impatient look came over Coryat's face. 'But I imagine you're not really interested in my career, Inspector. I understand you want my opinion on some pieces you've found.'

He went over to the desk in the window bay and pushed a few piles of papers aside to make space. 'I suggest you lay them out here.' He reached for the chain on the table lamp. A pool of ochre light fell on the desk's worn leather and mahogany surface.

De Silva opened the box he'd brought with him, took out the coins and the metal pieces and laid them on the desk. He watched as Coryat picked up each item in turn, weighed it in the palm of his hand and then peered at it through his spectacles. Eventually, he removed them and made a considerable business of polishing the lenses with a soft cloth. When he put the spectacles back on, it seemed he was still dissatisfied. 'Damned things,' he muttered. 'No use at all.'

'Perhaps you should buy some new ones, sir,' de Silva offered, trying to be helpful.

Coryat scowled. 'I already have, but I've mislaid them.'

He took a magnifying glass from a drawer and continued with his examination. For several minutes, there was no sound in the room apart from the tick of the clock on the mantelpiece. De Silva wrapped his arms across his chest and repressed a shiver. The room felt dank. If Coryat spent most of his waking hours in here, it was no wonder he was so lugubrious. De Silva couldn't remember when he had last seen such a cheerless place.

At last, Coryat put down his magnifying glass. He waved vaguely in the direction of the armchairs. 'Sit down; sit down. I need to look something up, but it won't take long.'

He went over to one of the bookcases; de Silva noticed how he fumbled with the small key to the glass door's lock before he managed to turn it. Running a crooked finger along the spines of the books, he selected the one he wanted and pulled it out then took it to his desk.

Another silence, this time only disturbed by the rustle

of pages. De Silva began to think this visit was going to be of very little value.

Coryat closed the book. 'Just as I thought. I'm sorry to be the bearer of bad tidings, Inspector, but none of your finds are of any importance. The coins are old and might fetch a few annas in one of the tourist markets in Colombo or Kandy, but you may as well dispose of the rest. These broken pieces would only be valuable if they came from something particularly rare or ancient. They don't.'

'But aren't they made of gold? Surely that makes them valuable?'

Coryat smiled for the first time. 'You're an optimist, I see. Not gold, the metal is an alloy. A little history lesson for you, Inspector: some two hundred years ago, a London clockmaker and jeweller called Pinchbeck invented a formula for an alloy of copper and zinc that resembled gold in virtually every respect except value. He called it Pinchbeck after himself and jewellery made from it became very popular in Victorian England among those who couldn't afford gold, or those who could, but wanted to leave their precious pieces safe at home when they travelled. As is the way of the world, Pinchbeck has had many imitators down the years. Your pieces are among them.'

He went to the bookcase and replaced the book. 'Where were these things found?'

While de Silva explained, Coryat rubbed the bridge of his long nose pensively. 'To the best of my knowledge, there have never been any excavations in that area,' he said when de Silva had finished. 'Is anything known about the man who was murdered?'

'Only that he occasionally worked as a tracker for foreign hunters.'

'Perhaps his activities extended to supplying the more insalubrious market traders with spurious "antiquities". They then sell them to gullible tourists looking for souvenirs. I've come across plenty of that type over the years. A few of them even had the brass neck to try and foist their wretched rubbish on the museum in Colombo when I was a senior curator there. I gave them short shrift, I can tell you.'

He glanced at de Silva. 'I'm sorry, Inspector, I see I'm not being much help to you.'

'Not at all, sir. I merely like to know what I'm dealing with in a case, and your opinion has given me that information.'

'Good.'

There was a pause. 'Forgive me not offering you refreshments,' Coryat resumed. 'I allow the servants to go to their quarters most of the time. An old bachelor like me doesn't need much doing for him, and I like my privacy. Servants fussing around are a distraction I can well do without.'

He led the way back to the front door and stood aside. 'I wish you a safe journey, Inspector.'

De Silva thanked him and stepped out onto the drive. He was glad that the sun had come out and it wasn't raining; he needed to banish the despondency Coryat's home had aroused. What a lonely life the man must lead. There had been no family photographs, nothing to indicate that Coryat cared to take part in the world outside his drab bungalow. Small wonder he had resisted Florence's blandishments.

He climbed into the car and started up the engine. He ought to stop at the station to check there was no news, but he would make the visit a brief one. He was looking forward to being home with Jane. As he so often did, he thought how lucky he was to have her and a home he loved. Poor old Coryat: all alone with his books and his dusty learning. De Silva wouldn't be in his shoes for all the world.

As he neared the gates, he saw a shack he hadn't noticed on the way up. Out of curiosity, he stopped and beckoned to the man who was lounging in the shade under the eaves of the thatched roof. He stood up slowly and came over to the car. 'Can I help you, sahib?' he asked in Tamil.

'Are you one of Sahib Coryat's servants?'

The man acknowledged it with a slight incline of his head.

'When did he last call you up to the bungalow?'

The man eyed him with suspicion.

'I am Inspector de Silva, here on police business.'

'I see, sahib.' The man thought for a moment. 'Two days ago. He needed some washing done. My wife saw to it and I took it back in the evening.'

'What about his meals?'

The man shrugged. 'My wife prepares food when he calls for it.'

'How often is that?'

'Different times.'

'But at least once a day?'

'Not every day.'

De Silva sighed inwardly. This wasn't getting him anywhere. Coryat was obviously a very unusual character. Most of the British were only too happy to be waited on hand and foot. It was hard to understand a man who cared so little for his own comfort.

CHAPTER 7

'You make it sound very bleak,' said Jane when he'd described Coryat's home, and what the servant had told him about his master's way of life.

'It certainly wouldn't do for me,' de Silva said with a grimace. Outside, the rain had started falling again and he was extremely glad to be back in the cosy drawing room at Sunnybank, especially with the prospect of a good dinner ahead. The only thing troubling him was that he wasn't sure where to go from here with the case.

'What do you plan to do next?' asked Jane.

He sighed. 'I'm not at all sure. I suppose I could speak to Velu's wife again; it's possible she's hiding something. Then there's the headman and the other villagers, but unless I can persuade any of them to speak frankly, I'll be relying on hunches to work out if one of them is guilty of murder.'

Jane smiled. 'Hunches have served you well in the past, dear.'

'I won't deny it, but this time I feel as if I'm up against a brick wall.'

'Are you convinced that this Mr Coryat knows his stuff?'

'Well, Archie Clutterbuck seems to think he does. Apparently, Coryat had a distinguished career in archaeology.'

'*Had*, dear.'

'What do you mean?'

'Well, from the way you described him, he does sound strange. These elderly academics can become very eccentric, you know; even a little soft in the head.'

'You mean he might be losing his skittles?'

'His marbles, dear.'

'Yes, well, I suppose that's possible.'

'If he is, it might be worth getting a second opinion. I must say, I am rather surprised that he dismissed everything so quickly.'

'A second opinion? Where do you suggest we go for that? I doubt there's another archaeologist for miles. Anyway, Archie Clutterbuck wasn't keen on spending much time on this.'

'What a pity. I was thinking of Kandy, or perhaps even Colombo. Maybe there's some way of persuading him. We haven't been away from Nuala for ages. We could combine a little holiday with your investigation.'

De Silva grinned. 'Ah, I see what this is about. You'd like a shopping trip.'

'Nonsense! I'm simply applying your own principle of no stone unturned. And if there happens to be time for shopping, it would be very pleasant.'

He put down his empty glass and stood up to plant a kiss on her forehead. 'I'm only teasing. If Archie can be made to come around to the idea, a visit to the museum in Colombo might be most instructive, and I certainly don't begrudge a little shopping along the way.'

'We'll have to be cautious though.'

'What do you mean?'

'If this Mr Coryat worked at the museum in Colombo, he may know people who are still there. We wouldn't want anything to get back to him, would we?'

De Silva scratched his chin. 'From the way he lives, it seems unlikely, but we certainly wouldn't. I'll have a think about how best to approach this.'

'What about making one more visit to the place where you found these things before we go? It would be rather exciting to do some more exploring.'

'Like in *King Solomon's Mines*?' Recently, they had both read Rider Haggard's adventure story.

'Yes, but hopefully we won't get lost. I think we should take Prasanna and Nadar too. That way we can cover more ground in less time.'

De Silva raised an eyebrow. 'My goodness, you have it all worked out. I think I may as well retire and let you take charge.'

'Certainly not. I have far too many other things going on,' said Jane airily. 'For instance, how would the sewing circle survive without me?'

'And who else would keep Florence Clutterbuck in order?'

She laughed. 'I doubt I do that, but it's kind of you to give me the credit. Actually, there'll be no need of it for a while. Did I tell you she's off on a cruise?'

'Good gracious! Florence on a cruise. Is there a ship sturdy enough?'

'Shanti! That's unkind.'

'Sorry, I was just joking.' He gave her a shrewd look. 'But is that another reason for you wanting a holiday?'

Jane sniffed. 'If you're implying I feel the need to keep up with her, I certainly don't.'

He patted her hand. 'We'll have our holiday, I promise. I'd enjoy it as much as you would.'

CHAPTER 8

When de Silva went to make his report to Archie Clutter-buck the following morning, he found that the Residence's usually calm conduct of affairs had been replaced by a scene of chaos. The portico's broad stone steps played haughty host to a profusion of trunks, bags and hatboxes. Florence, dressed in a light-brown travelling suit, stood amid them, directing the show with her customary imperiousness.

As de Silva approached the steps, the small creature that unfailingly reminded him of an animated household mop scampered out of the building, weaving through the luggage.

'Angel!' shrieked Florence. 'Come back at once!'

De Silva scooped up the black-and-white shih tzu and carried him to his mistress.

'Oh, thank you, Inspector.'

She tapped Angel's black button of a nose. 'Naughty! We have to leave soon, so no running away.'

'Are you off on your travels, ma'am?'

'I'm going up to Trincomalee. My nephew's stationed at the Naval Base there. He commands a destroyer, you know.'

De Silva hadn't known, but he smiled to be polite.

'He's promised me a tour of the Grand Harbour which I'm greatly looking forward to. I'm told it's magnificent. Have you been there, Inspector?'

'I've never had the pleasure, ma'am. You'll come back far better acquainted with my country than me.'

Briefly, he wondered whether he had made an unfortunate remark. It was debatable, of course, whose country Ceylon was, although he liked to regard himself as having a greater entitlement to it than the British, at least on historical grounds. Fortunately, Florence was too full of her plans to take umbrage.

'We are all guilty of that to some extent, Inspector,' she said equably. 'There are many parts of England I've never visited. When my husband retires, it would be pleasant to remedy that.'

'And I trust you will, ma'am. But I hope it will be many years before you are taken away from us,' he added quickly.

'My nephew has leave due to him, so he and his wife will come up to Jaffna with me. I have old friends there whom Archie and I knew from our Colombo days when we were new to the Service. It's a great pity he's unable to come with me, but the poor man is so busy.'

Wryly, de Silva speculated that Archie would be rather looking forward to some peace and quiet.

'After that, we'll be taking a cruise for a few weeks. I must say, I'll be glad to be away from this tiresome weather. In all the years we've lived here, I've never become resigned to it.'

De Silva smiled. 'Having two monsoon seasons is most convenient, ma'am. It's dry in the north and east when it's wet here and in the west.'

While Florence had been distracted by what was probably one of the longest conversations she and de Silva had ever conducted, as opposed to him listening to one of her monologues, the Residence staff had managed to stow all her luggage in the official car. Two of them remained standing by the steps, awaiting further orders. Florence's gimlet eye swept over them. For their sakes, de Silva hoped she would find everything in order.

Archie Clutterbuck emerged from the house, Darcy at his heels. 'Morning, de Silva!'

He turned to his wife. 'Are you ready for the off, my dear?'

'Nearly. But I sent the maid in for my hat and my handbag, and I can't think where she's got to. Would you mind, dear?'

'Of course not.'

He went back into the house but was out again a moment later with the maid in his wake, carrying the bag and a stylish cloche hat that was soon settled on Florence's head. She proffered her cheek, and he planted a rather awkward kiss on it. 'Take care, my dear,' he said as he straightened up.

She patted his arm. 'I will. I'll send a telegram to let you know we've arrived safely.'

He nodded.

De Silva felt somewhat guilty. He hoped he wasn't being a raspberry at this leave-taking – or was it a gooseberry? He must ask Jane. But neither of the Clutterbucks seemed inclined to linger. Florence was soon ensconced in the official car's back seat with the household mop on her lap, and her maid in front with the chauffeur.

'They've plenty of time to get to the station at Nanu Oya,' Clutterbuck remarked. 'But they'll need it with all that luggage to load on the train. Beats me why my wife needs to take so much; I suppose some is gifts for her hosts. She insisted on taking them tea – says it tastes better when it comes straight from the plantation rather than via the auctions at Colombo.'

He raised a hand and waved as the official car glided down the drive, slowed to go between the wrought-iron gates, and turned onto the road.

'Well,' he said briskly. 'You'd better come inside and tell me how you got on with old Coryat.'

* * *

Clutterbuck leant back in his chair, rested his elbows on the desk and pressed the tips of his fingers together.

'Fire away.'

'Mr Coryat wasn't impressed with what I had to show him, I'm afraid. It was his opinion that none of the pieces were of any value. He also said he wasn't aware of there ever having been excavations in that area. He suggested that the pieces might have been in Velu's possession because he was hoping to sell them to unscrupulous market traders who would sell them on to gullible tourists looking for souvenirs.'

Clutterbuck reached for his cigarettes and lit up a Passing Cloud.

'Plausible, I suppose,' he said, shaking out the match and dropping it in the ashtray on his desk. 'Perhaps Velu had an accomplice, and there was an argument that got out of hand. What do you think?'

De Silva hesitated for a moment. On reflection, he had no good reason to doubt Henry Coryat's capabilities, and the idea that he had lost his marbles wasn't a serious one. Clutterbuck might well take a dim view of a local policeman questioning the opinion of someone the British regarded as an authority in his field. He'd have to tread carefully.

Clutterbuck exhaled a puff of smoke. 'Well, out with it,' he said, in an encouraging tone. 'It's many moons since I saw old Coryat. I'm interested in your opinion of him. A man can go a bit doolally when he's too much in his own company, you know. Do you think he's still all there?'

De Silva smiled. 'He certainly didn't seem mad, and I'm sure his opinion was based on a great deal of knowledge and experience, but nevertheless, we have so little else to go on that I'm unwilling to close off the line of investigation just yet.'

'What did you have in mind?'

Deciding not to mention the idea of a second opinion for the moment, de Silva drew a breath. 'I'd like to spend some more time searching the area where we found Velu's body. Even if the pieces I showed to Coryat are valueless, that doesn't mean to say that Velu didn't have others that are valuable.'

'I'll grant you that. I happened to be talking with Charlie Frobisher yesterday – the young fellow who helped you out on the old Hatton road. He saw you leaving the Residence after our meeting and asked how you were faring. I mentioned the business of this man Velu and your finds, and he was intrigued. It turns out he has an enthusiasm for archaeology. His grandfather was a keen amateur archaeologist and when he heard Frobisher was coming out here, he was very interested. He told Frobisher about a Victorian traveller who came to the Nuala area with the intention of doing a bit of treasure hunting.'

'Did he find anything, sir?'

'Not a scrap. Poor fellow died from a snakebite soon after he went into the jungle. He'd been the moving spirit and without him, the expedition collapsed. The locals dispersed, and his British companion returned home in poor health after contracting a fever.'

De Silva shuddered at the mention of death by snakebite.

'The companion never fully recovered and died a year after reaching home, but by then he had returned her husband's effects to the widow,' Clutterbuck went on. 'There were diaries among them that Frobisher now has. There was some family connection, I believe, but he can tell you more about that himself.'

He glanced out of the window. Dark clouds massed behind the belt of trees beyond the lawn. 'When do you plan to make this search? The rain won't hold off much longer. I suggest we see what the weather's like in the morning then decide how to proceed.'

De Silva was taken aback. Archie wanted to come too? Usually the only activities that inveigled him from the

Residence were hunting, fishing, and golf. Was he developing a sense of adventure? Or had he always had one, but it had been held in check by his wife's presence?

'No need to look so bemused, de Silva. I won't get in your way, but Frobisher piqued my interest. I want to see what you find first-hand. Frobisher will join us.'

'Very good, sir.'

'We'll speak in the morning. Oh, I almost forgot. The headman of the village where Velu lived appears to have a blameless record. My officials tell me he's always had a reputation for paying the village taxes on time, and there've been no complaints about him from his villagers.'

That didn't mean to say that they had no grievances, thought de Silva; merely that none had ever been reported. But it provided some reassurance that he would be dealing with an honest man.

'Thank you, sir. That's helpful. I'll go over there this afternoon and see what I can find out.'

'Good.'

Clutterbuck stubbed out his cigarette and got to his feet. 'Until tomorrow then.'

CHAPTER 9

'Do you think Archie read *King Solomon's Mines* as a boy?' asked de Silva as he and Jane ate in the dining room. The clouds had opened on his way home to Sunnybank, and lunch on the verandah hadn't seemed an appealing prospect. He ladled sambar into a bowl and topped the hot, spicy concoction with a couple of rice patties. He rubbed his hands. 'Just what's needed on such a dreary afternoon.'

'I doubt there are many Englishmen of his stamp who didn't,' replied Jane with a laugh. 'I agree it's unusual for him to want to be personally involved in an investigation, so you're probably right he's attracted by the prospect of an adventure. I'm sure lots of Englishmen have harboured a secret desire to be Allan Quatermain and find lost cities of gold. It's the kind of romantic notion that helped to build the British Empire.'

'Particularly the prospect of the gold,' de Silva said wryly. 'But I must admit, it's somewhat galling that it was his talk with Charlie Frobisher rather than anything I said that interested him in this expedition.'

'You can't assume that, dear. Anyway, you've got the result you wanted, whatever brought it about. And even if you're right, it may not all have been down to Frobisher. I expect Archie's rather bored too. Thanks to the monsoon, his beloved outdoor pursuits have to take a back seat, and we know he's not much of a man for reading.'

'He does have his job to do.'

'Yes, but that doesn't take up every minute of the day.'

'That's true.'

He finished off the sambar and rice then dabbed his lips with his napkin. 'Excellent. Well, so long as he doesn't expect me to play the noble savage, Umbopa, to his British Allan Quatermain, I don't mind him coming along. It will be useful to have another pair of eyes, and Charlie Frobisher may prove to be a positive asset.'

A servant came in to clear the plates and bring more rice and an array of curries.

'Archie wants me to telephone him in the morning,' de Silva said. 'We'll decide then if the weather's good enough to go. Meanwhile, I'll drive over to Velu's village this afternoon and see if I can find out anything that might help us.'

Jane frowned. 'In this rain, dear?'

He sniffed the delicious aroma of his favourite cashew and pea curry and piled some onto his plate. 'If everything came to a halt because of the monsoon, we'd get nothing done from May to September. Don't worry; I'm used to it.'

* * *

After a short nap, he drove to the police station and collected Prasanna. It would be handy to have him along to help find the way to the village – hopefully, in this weather, they wouldn't need to walk too far from the road. It would also be useful to have Prasanna to smooth the path for the interview he hoped to have with Kuveni's brother, Vijay, if they could find him. What the headman and the other villagers had to say might be important, but Vijay had worked with the dead man. He might even have been the last person to see him alive.

In the few days since he had last driven along it, the

monsoon rain had washed away more of the run-down surface of the old Hatton road. De Silva was glad that Gopallawa hadn't telephoned to say the Morris was repaired. The borrowed car had its vices, including a tendency for the gear stick to jam between the second and third gears and a persistent leak where one of the windows didn't roll up properly, but he had far fewer qualms about subjecting it to this rough road than he would have done with the Morris.

The drive was a tedious one. Although his cold had seemed to be on the wane that morning, by the time they reached the spot where Prasanna advised leaving the car, de Silva had a headache from staring into the curtains of rain that reduced visibility to a quarter of the distance he felt comfortable with.

He pulled the car off the road and Prasanna ran to the boot and fetched the raingear they had brought with them. Struggling against the wind, they donned it and set off.

De Silva had to keep a hand on his hat to stop it being blown away, and the wind buffeted his raincoat so that it constantly flapped against his legs and impeded him. The steaming, milky air caught in his throat; his body heat trapped by the raingear, he started to sweat profusely. He scowled as water streamed from the brim of his hat, some of it finding its ingenious way under his collar. Enviously, he looked at Prasanna who was making much lighter work of the journey than he was. Oh, to be a young man again.

'Is it much further?' he shouted over the wind and rain.

'No, nearly there, sir. At the top of this slope, we're on the edge of the village.'

They ploughed on, the cleats of de Silva's rubber boots by now so clogged with mud and mashed up fallen leaves that it seemed to him they weighed twice as much as they had when he first put them on. He consoled himself with the thought that at least no snakes would be out of their burrows in this weather.

At last, to his relief, the shape of a thatched hut loomed out of the murk. Soon, they were at the centre of the small village. De Silva went over to the largest hut, presuming it to be the headman's. He twitched aside the canvas curtain hanging across the doorway.

'Hello?'

There were rustling sounds inside, then a series of coughs. He called again.

'Who is it?' grumbled a man's voice.

'Police.'

A moment passed then an elderly man came to the door and pulled back the curtain. He wore long, loose trousers and a bulky, dun-coloured woollen jumper, but his feet were bare. In contrast, the woollen hat pulled well down over his ears was as red as a cockscomb. Below it, his eyes had a wary expression.

'Are you the headman here?'

The elderly man nodded.

'Can we come in? We mean you no harm. I need to ask you some questions.'

Reluctantly, the headman stood aside for them to enter.

It took a few moments for de Silva's eyes to become accustomed to the gloom. When they were, he saw there were two young men in the room as well as three women, two of them young and one middle-aged, also numerous children. If any of them recognised Prasanna, they didn't acknowledge him.

The back of the room was taken up by a clutch of pallet beds. Next to one of them stood a crudely fashioned wooden cradle. Fetid air, stale cooking smells and the aroma of unwashed bodies made de Silva's nose twitch. A bleating sound indicated that the family goats, presumably too valuable to be left out in the rain, were also somewhere inside the hut.

The cradle suddenly emitted a loud wail. The headman

barked an order to one of the women who went to pick up the baby and put it to her breast.

'Tell me then,' he said gruffly. 'What has my grandson done?'

De Silva saw the middle-aged woman pull the edge of her sari across to hide her face. He heard her weeping.

'Your grandson?' he asked with a frown. 'I haven't come about your grandson. I'm here to make inquiries about a man called Velu.'

The wariness faded from the man's eyes. 'Velu? He hasn't been here for many days. What do you want with him?'

'I'll come to that. First, tell me what kind of man he is.'

'Not a good one. He's lazy and likes to quarrel.' He pointed to the prettier of the young women. 'He wanted to marry my granddaughter, but I told him no. Later, he stole grain from me.'

'Do you have proof of that?'

'He denied it, but all the other villagers can be trusted.'

De Silva let the summary judgement pass. It didn't matter to Velu now.

'Are any of his family in the village?'

De Silva partly knew the answer, but he wanted to see if the headman confirmed that the woman who claimed to be Velu's widow had told the truth. It wasn't unknown for people to pretend they had lost a relative to get help. Kuveni might have been lied to as well.

'He has a wife, but she is unhappy with him. He never gives her money. She grows vegetables on their plot and sells them in exchange for rice and eggs.'

'Has Velu talked of leaving the village for good?'

The headman shrugged. 'He's hardly here anyway.'

'Where does he go?'

Another shrug. 'He never says. And when I tell him that if he doesn't work his patch of land, I'll give it and his hut to a family who need it, he laughs and boasts he'll soon have somewhere much better to live.'

'What about his wife? How would she live?'

'As a servant in Nuala perhaps? Who can say?'

What an unpleasant man, thought de Silva. The British might be happy with the way he ran his village, but there was no kindness in him.

The middle-aged woman had stopped weeping, and she and the younger two were now huddled by the back wall of the hut, whispering to each other. The young men watched the proceedings with mild interest.

'But why are you asking about Velu, sahib?' the headman asked.

'He's been murdered. His body was found in the jungle near here.'

A gasp came from the women, but the young men and the headman seemed unperturbed. 'Then I can give his hut and his land to someone else,' said the latter, a note of satisfaction in his voice.

'Not before my sergeant and I have had time to search it,' said de Silva firmly. 'Get one of your boys to take us there now.'

The headman nodded to one of the young men. 'My son will take you.'

Truculently, the headman's son went to the door and waited for de Silva and Prasanna to follow.

'Before we go,' said de Silva, 'what's this about your grandson?'

'Nothing.'

'It must be something, or why did you ask what he'd done this time?'

The headman was tight-lipped. De Silva looked at the women, but they avoided his eye.

'You may as well tell me now. I won't go anywhere until I have an answer.'

'There was some trouble in Hatton,' the headman started

reluctantly. 'Bad men said my grandson was involved, but the British magistrate didn't find him guilty of any crime. He was set free.'

'But he's not here now. Do you know where he is?'

'Perhaps he has found work in Hatton.'

'Why would he do that and not tell you?'

The headman raised an eyebrow and pointed a bony finger at the middle-aged woman who began to cry again. 'Ask her, she is his mother, the widow of my son by my first wife. Maybe he was tired of her complaining,' he added viciously.

The woman hung her head. Her young companions made sympathetic noises that seemed to infuriate the headman. 'Enough!' he snapped. 'Was there ever a man as unlucky with his wives as I am? The mother of these boys,' he gestured to the two young men, 'died complaining as well.'

'We haven't come to listen to your family troubles,' de Silva said sharply. The headman might be praiseworthy in his public life, but if, as appeared to be the case, his private one left much to be desired, it was spiteful of him to air it to strangers.

He went to the door where the headman's son waited. 'We're wasting time. Take us to Velu's hut now.'

Back out in the rain, they squelched across what seemed to be the central path through the village onto a narrower one. The huts looked much poorer and many of their thatched roofs showed signs of rot. There was no one about apart from a few rangy dogs scavenging in the gully that ran along one side of the path and some disconsolate chickens penned up in crates placed on their sides and turned into coops by pieces of wire tacked over the openings.

Velu's hut was neat but as dispiriting as the rest. Steady drips plopped from several holes in the banana-leaf thatch through which appeared gunmetal sky. A tin can, charred from use as a cooking utensil, contained the remains of a meal. De Silva sighed. He felt even more sorry for Velu's wife than he had before. The picture of her life that was emerging was a grim one.

'Thank you, you may take us back now.'

They splashed back to the main area of the village. De Silva gave the headman's son a few annas which brightened his expression.

'Do you know how to get to Nuala?' de Silva asked. The young man nodded. 'If later, there is anything you think I might like to know about Velu, come and find me at the police station and there will be more for you.'

'Do you think they're telling the truth, sir?' asked Prasanna as the young man went back into the headman's hut.

'Hard to say, but it certainly sounds as if no one liked this Velu much. If that man was right, probably his widow's more concerned about the loss of her home than the loss of her husband.'

'That's the impression Kuveni and I also have, sir.'

'It's kind of you to take care of her.'

'She's a good woman and industrious. It's not a hardship for us.'

'I'm glad to hear it. I'd like to speak to Kuveni's brother now. Can you find him for me? After that, we may as well head for home.'

The hut where Kuveni's brother, Vijay, and their father lived was on the far side of the village at a short distance from the others in that area. It would be a long time, if ever, de Silva reflected, before the Vedda people were fully accepted by their Tamil and Sinhalese compatriots.

De Silva and Prasanna were far more welcome guests there. They spoke in Sinhalese, halting on Vijay's part, and sometimes Prasanna had to help by translating words into the Vedda language he had learnt from Kuveni. De Silva had the impression the old father was taking in very little, but he seemed content to sit quietly, occasionally nodding.

Prasanna produced a small bottle from his pocket and gave it to Vijay. 'Kuveni sent this for your father. It will help him to breathe more easily. She got it from the British doctor.'

Vijay took the bottle and said something to his father in Vedda. The old man eyed the bottle suspiciously as Prasanna explained how the medicine should be taken. De Silva wondered if he would use it or simply wait until Prasanna had gone then resort to whatever potion the village herbalist advised. He feared that nothing was likely to make a great deal of difference to the old man in any case. He looked extremely frail, his body wasted and his eyes dull. When he coughed, which he did frequently, de Silva heard his chest rattle.

They came to the subject of Velu, and, when he heard that the man was dead, Vijay looked alarmed.

'No one is blaming you,' said de Silva hastily. 'But I hope you can help us with our inquiries. How well did you know him?'

'We worked together five or six times.'

'Tracking for game hunters?'

Vijay looked down and scuffed the earth floor with his foot.

'Yes,' he muttered.

'Don't worry. I'm not concerned about whether it was illegal or not, although I advise you not to make a habit of breaking the law.'

'Thank you, sahib.'

'Did he tell you much about his life?'

'He had harsh words for the headman, and he complained about his wife, but many men grumble.'

Prasanna grinned. 'Not about your sister.'

Vijay returned the grin. 'Kuveni is an angel.'

'The headman told us Velu spent a lot of time away from the village,' said de Silva, wanting to keep the conversation on track. 'If he wasn't working with you, do you have any idea what he was doing?'

Vijay shrugged. 'Working for other hunters maybe. He always talked about hunters and the work he did for them. And about the big tips they gave him,' he added wryly. 'The rest of us didn't believe everything he said.'

'A boastful man, eh?'

'Yes, but he liked to laugh and joke too.'

'As far as you know, had he any enemies?'

'Some people got angry with his big talk, but most didn't mind.'

De Silva sighed inwardly. He didn't really know what he had expected, but this trip to the village certainly wasn't proving very illuminating.

'We'd better be getting along,' he said to Prasanna, after a few more questions had been equally unfruitful. 'I'd like to get back to Nuala before nightfall.'

They said goodbye and went out into the rain once more. The wind had gathered strength and was lashing the trees. The ceaseless motion of the jungle canopy made de Silva feel he was on a stormy sea. The thought of Florence, enjoying the sunshine in Trincomalee, popped into his mind.

When they reached the car, the force of the wind almost pulled the door out of his hand as he opened it. Once safe inside, he and Prasanna struggled out of their sopping raingear and bundled it into the passenger footwell. Prasanna crouched in his seat, rubbing his hands together to warm them. His dark hair was plastered to his head and his clothes were damp right through; de Silva knew he was in no better state.

'I'm so wet, I shall have to wring myself out like a rag before Mrs de Silva lets me in the house,' he remarked.

Prasanna chuckled. 'Kuveni too, sir.'

De Silva turned the key. He hoped the journey back to Nuala wouldn't be a disaster like his earlier one on this road.

CHAPTER 10

Fortunately, they met no obstacles on the way, and, a couple of hours later, he reached Sunnybank, having deposited Prasanna close to his home. The report of the day's work would have to wait. De Silva wanted a hot bath.

Luxuriating in the steaming water, he considered how the case was progressing. Had the villagers been lying to him? He had no evidence they were, but murder was a convenient way of disposing of an unpopular man. It would be interesting to see who ended up with Velu's hut. It was hardly a great prize, yet a villager with no home of his own might be tempted to commit a crime to win it.

The absence of the headman's grandson raised more questions. As the lad had been up before the Hatton magistrate, maybe he would telephone Inspector Singh down there and find out what he had to say about the boy.

Lastly, there was Vijay. He hadn't liked to say anything to Prasanna on the way home, but one couldn't dismiss the possibility that the work he and Velu had done together hadn't always been tracking. If there had been other activities, was Vijay covering up a crime? Might there even have been a reason why he wanted Velu dead? Kuveni's brother didn't look like a murderer, but one could never tell. For Kuveni's sake, he hoped he was wrong, but, at this stage, he couldn't rule Vijay out.

Sitting up, he reached for the soap, lathered himself

vigorously and then slid under the water once more for a final soak. When the water started to cool, he climbed out and rubbed himself dry, then wrapped the towel round his middle and padded to the bedroom. Jane must have heard him for she came in and sat down on the bed.

'Feeling better, dear?'

'Infinitely. Nothing like a hot bath.'

'Was the visit worth the effort?'

'I wouldn't say I learnt a great deal, but there's a new lead to follow up.'

He explained about the headman's grandson; he wouldn't mention Vijay for the moment. Jane would be upset for Kuveni's sake.

'It's too late to catch Inspector Singh,' he went on. 'They'll have shut up shop at Hatton by now. I'll call in the morning.'

Jane stood up. 'Good. I need a word with Cook about dinner. I'd better go and do that, then I'll see you in the drawing room.'

After she'd gone, de Silva dressed quickly. Enough thinking about Velu's case for tonight, he resolved. He would enjoy his dinner and take a fresh look at what little he had to go on in the morning. The happy thought occurred to him that this expedition into the jungle might be the adventure that changed everything.

* * *

The following day, however, the rain was heavy. De Silva passed the time writing up his report of the visit to the village and putting other paperwork in order, a job that was not one of his favourite pastimes but had to be done occasionally. He also telephoned his counterpart in Hatton, Inspector Singh.

'I know the lad you're talking about,' said the inspector. 'He's been in trouble a few times, but murder? I'd be very surprised. So far, his offences have been minor, although I suppose it's possible he's got in with a bad crowd. It's never hard for that to happen.'

De Silva remembered the boy's weeping mother. He wondered whether he should have asked her more questions. Maybe he would go back to the village one day and see if he could speak to her on her own. She might respond to assurances that he wanted to help her son stay out of trouble. It sounded like he wasn't the killer, but if he had got in with the wrong crowd, he might have an idea who was, and why the crime had been committed.

'Anyway, we'll keep an eye out for him,' Singh went on. 'If he turns up, I'll keep hold of him until you get down here.'

'Thank you, that would be a great help.'

'How's the case coming along?'

'It's a tricky one. Right now, there's not much to go on.'

'Well, good luck. I'll be in touch.'

'I hope so.'

* * *

Mid-morning on the next day, he received a call from Gopallawa Motors to say that the Morris was ready to be delivered. Should the driver bring it to the police station or to Sunnybank? De Silva had already decided to go home at lunchtime, so he told them to bring it to the bungalow.

Jane was lunching out and spending the rest of the afternoon at her sewing circle. Without her company, de Silva didn't linger over his meal. He hadn't long finished when the doorbell rang; he heard one of the servants speaking to the caller and went into the hall to join them.

'Good afternoon, sahib.'

De Silva recognised the mechanic from Gopallawa Motors. 'She's running perfectly now, sahib,' he said, handing over the keys. 'Do you wish to take a drive to satisfy yourself?'

Peering at the rain that continued to hiss down, creating shallow puddles on the gravel drive, de Silva shook his head. 'No need. I'll soon be on the telephone to your boss if there's a problem.'

'There won't be, sahib, I am confident of that.'

'Good. Have you brought the bill?'

'Here it is, sahib.'

'Tell your boss I'll settle it when I'm passing.'

'I'll tell him, sahib.'

When he had handed over the keys to the borrowed car, de Silva closed the door and went back to the drawing room. He sat down and cast his eye over the bill. Gopallawa was a bit of an old rogue but the charge didn't seem too unreasonable. He probably expected to be beaten down a few pounds all the same, and de Silva wasn't going to disappoint him, but it would have to wait a day or two. A trip into town wasn't an appealing prospect today.

He yawned. Jane was unlikely to be back much before dinner time. Maybe he'd spend the rest of the afternoon reading. Going to the bookshelves, he searched for *King Solomon's Mines*. Most of the books on the shelves were Jane's, but *King Solomon's Mines* was one of his, presented to him as a school prize. How many years ago was that? More than he liked to remember. He took the book over to his armchair and settled down to reread it.

* * *

It wasn't until one of the servants came in to serve tea that he realised he had been engrossed in the story for over two hours, living the hardships and dangers of Allan Quatermain and his comrades as they journeyed to find King Solomon's fabled diamond mines.

He put the book aside and set about eating his tea. Munching a slice of butter cake, he pondered the feelings the book aroused in him. Inevitably, there was plenty with which to find fault. He deplored the passages that glorified the hunting of elephants for their ivory, even though he was aware that, when the book was written in Victorian days, even more than today, no one questioned the morality of it. The narrator's, and by extension the author's, unquestioning assumption of the superiority of the white man over the rest of humanity grated too, even if Rider Haggard did have the grace to praise the courage and skill in warfare of the natives of the fictional Kukuanaland.

Undeniably, though, Haggard spun a good yarn; the story thrived on action and adventure. Yet at times, Haggard allowed his hero a moment of reflection. Then there were passages of prose that verged on poetry and compelled de Silva to go back and read them again. Quatermain, the narrator, was a bluff adventurer who prided himself on his ability to survive in the harshest of circumstances, but he also appreciated beauty. His description of the great ice cavern at the entrance to the treasure chamber, where the slow drip of water had, over the centuries, formed stalactites and stalagmites that eventually met, creating gigantic columns as awe-inspiring as those of any medieval cathedral, was thrilling. Quatermain's meditation on the fate of the thousands of warriors who fell in the battle for Kukuanaland also surprised de Silva. He read it once more:

Only the old moon would shine on serenely, the night wind would stir the grasses, and the wide earth would take its rest, even as it did aeons before we were, and will do aeons after we have been forgotten.

Yet man dies not whilst the world, at once his mother and his monument, remains, His name is lost, indeed, but the breath he breathed still stirs the pine tops on the mountains, the sound of the words he spoke yet echoes on through space; the thoughts his brain gave birth to we have inherited today; his passions are our cause of life; the joys and sorrows that he knew are our familiar friends – the end from which he fled aghast will surely overtake us also!

Truly the universe is full of ghosts, not sheeted churchyard spectres, but the inextinguishable elements of individual life, which having once been, can never die, though they blend and change, and change again forever.

The book resting in his lap, de Silva pondered those words. Velu had gone to join that great company of spirits; had he left behind echoes of his life that would reveal the secret of his fate?

Unburdened of his philosophical thoughts, Quatermain had resumed the role of man of action, regretting that "the detestable habit of thinking" seemed to be getting hold of him. Action not contemplation: it was the secret of British success. Wherever the British went, they brought their urge to build and organise with them. In some respects, it was an excellent thing, yet there were times when it sowed discord.

He glanced out of the window. It was already dusk. Was it his imagination, or was the rain slackening? Tomorrow was Sunday. Clutterbuck would probably insist they waited until Monday now, but then they might have some action of their own.

CHAPTER 11

To his relief, Monday morning dawned clear and bright, the sky a soft, pale blue that was a welcome change from the louring grey of the last two days. Jane and de Silva were still eating breakfast when the telephone rang in the hall. A servant went to answer it then came into the dining room.

'It is a call from the Residence, sahib.'

De Silva wiped egg from his lips and pushed back his chair. 'I'll come.'

Jane smiled. 'It sounds like Archie's eager for his adventure.'

His ear to the telephone, de Silva waited a moment while the Residence's telephonist transferred the call.

'De Silva?' Clutterbuck's voice boomed down the line. 'Perfect morning for it. I think we should get off as soon as possible before the dratted rain comes in again.'

'I agree, sir.'

'I'll meet you at the police station in an hour then we can drive in convoy; less likely to miss each other that way.'

'Very well, my men and I will be waiting. My wife has also offered to help.'

There was a pause at the other end of the line, and de Silva grimaced. Was Archie going to take the same stand as Allan Quatermain – *no petticoats welcome*? It was going to be difficult to mediate between him and Jane if that was the case. Fortunately, he soon realised that it wasn't Archie's intention to exclude her.

'I'll bring the Hillman estate,' he said cheerfully. 'Plenty of room in that.'

De Silva returned to the dining room and sat down to finish his breakfast.

'Everything in order, dear?'

'It seems so. Archie sounded very bullish. He's going to meet us at the station in an hour. He says he'll have plenty of room in his car. Prasanna and Nadar will be pleased. They were expecting to have to use their bicycles.'

'Gracious, it sounds as if he's not planning to stand on ceremony. I wonder how Prasanna and Nadar will take to riding in one of the Residence's cars.'

'I expect they'll find it somewhat daunting but easier on the legs.'

Jane drank the last of her tea and put the cup back on the saucer. 'I'd better go and get ready.'

'Don't be too long.'

'I won't.'

She returned a quarter of an hour later dressed in a pair of light-brown cotton trousers and a jacket of the same material over a plain white shirt. On her feet, she wore a pair of sturdy walking boots.

'Will I do?'

De Silva chuckled. 'Are we going to a fashion parade?'

She pulled a face. 'You know what I mean – are these clothes suitable?'

'Of course, and you look very nice in them too. I'm not used to seeing you in trousers. You'll need a hat.'

'I have one.'

The drive to the station didn't take long. They found Prasanna and Nadar already there. A few minutes later, a rather elderly Hillman estate car pulled up outside. De Silva was surprised to see that Clutterbuck, not one of the Residence staff, was at the wheel. His passengers were Darcy the Labrador and Charlie Frobisher.

In his early twenties, Frobisher was an athletic-looking young man with fair, curly hair and blue eyes that were currently screwed up against the morning sun. He put out a hand and shook de Silva's with a firm grip. 'Good morning, Inspector. I hope you don't object to my coming along.'

'Not at all, sir. An extra pair of eyes will be most welcome.'

'I take it your wife will ride with you, de Silva,' said Clutterbuck. He nodded to Prasanna and Nadar who were standing watching the proceedings with diffident expressions on their faces. 'You men can travel in the back of my car. Hop to it.'

He turned to de Silva. 'What equipment do you have on board?'

'Some spades, sir, and sticks for beating down the undergrowth. And bags in case we find anything we want to bring back as evidence.'

'I've taken the precaution of bringing a lot more than that.'

Clutterbuck went to the back of the Hillman and opened the doors of the boot to reveal a veritable arsenal of spades, pickaxes, trowels, buckets, and even a large coil of sturdy rope, along with several food hampers. Clearly, he didn't intend going hungry. De Silva wondered what was in those hampers. He had once shared some of the pork pies made by the Residence's cook with Clutterbuck, and they had been quite appetising, although the flavour was rather bland for his taste. He had also, however, experienced potted meat and tinned pilchards: both a crime against human taste buds.

With amusement, he speculated as to whether Prasanna and Nadar were in for their first encounter with those dubious British delicacies. If they were, he felt sorry for them. Luckily, at his request, Sunnybank's cook had supplied rotis, samosas, vegetable rolls, and egg and sambol buns as well as sandwiches for his and Jane's picnic. He had better offer Prasanna and Nadar some.

With Clutterbuck leading, they were soon on their way. He drove at a faster speed than de Silva would have chosen, but pride dictated that he didn't fall behind.

Jane wound down her window and rested her arm on the sill. 'What a lovely breeze.'

'Yes,' muttered de Silva. 'But I'd like to get there in one piece, and I expect Prasanna and Nadar would too.'

'Oh, don't worry, dear, I'm sure we will. I have complete faith in your driving.'

'Good of you to say so, but it's Archie's driving I'm bothered about.'

'I must admit, I never expected him to dash along like this. Florence's absence must have brought out the daredevil in him.'

De Silva chuckled.

When they reached the spot on the road close to where Velu's body had been found, the way Prasanna and Nadar stumbled from the Hillman's back seat indicated that they had been less sanguine. Charlie Frobisher, on the other hand, seemed unperturbed as he and Archie walked over to the Morris. Presumably, he was used to his boss's driving.

Clutterbuck tugged at the collar of his shirt. 'Dashed sticky out here. I suggest we don't stay more than a couple of hours.'

He turned to Jane. 'I expect you'd prefer to walk with your husband, Mrs de Silva. The rest of us will fan out to cover as much ground as possible. We'll start from the spot where you found the body, de Silva.'

Deciding to resign himself to the fact that Clutterbuck would instinctively take charge, de Silva nodded.

Loaded up with implements for digging, they were soon striking out into the trees. After a while, Charlie Frobisher fell into step with de Silva and Jane.

'I believe I have you to thank for promoting this expedition to our mutual boss, Mr Frobisher,' said de Silva.

Frobisher seemed a pleasant young man and he had done de Silva a good turn that night on the road from Hatton. De Silva felt rather churlish now for resenting his influence with Archie.

'Oh, call me Charlie, please. And I didn't do anything much. I just told him what I knew about Thomas Henchard.'

'The Victorian gentleman whose diaries you have?'

'Yes. Henchard's family lived in the same village in England as my people did. Henchard came out here in 1865, coincidentally the year of my grandfather's birth. After poor Henchard died, his widow remained in the village. She had no children, and when my grandfather was a boy, she became very fond of him. When he developed an interest in archaeology, she gave him her late husband's diaries.'

'How old would your grandfather have been then?' asked Jane.

'About sixteen, I believe.' Frobisher pushed a lock of fair hair out of his eyes. 'My father died in the Great War, and my mother needed to work, so I spent a lot of my childhood with my grandparents. It's from my grandfather that I get my interest in archaeology. He never managed to come to Ceylon, although he took a great interest in the country because of the connection to Thomas Henchard. He was very excited when he heard I had the chance to work here. He brought out the diaries and other papers he'd been given by old Mrs Henchard. We talked about them and Henchard's travels. My grandfather was convinced that if Henchard had lived, he would have unearthed marvellous things in the Nuala area.'

They reached the place where Velu's body had been found. The shallow grave still gaped at the sky.

Jane shuddered. 'What a dreadful place,' she whispered. 'I hate to think of that poor man dying such a violent death out here.'

'Your sentiments do you credit, my love, but I think I'll save my sympathy until we know why he was killed. There might be someone else more deserving of it.'

Clutterbuck sifted through a pile of dead leaves near the grave with his stick. De Silva noticed that it was rather a splendid one with a silver finial in the shape of a Labrador's head.

'I take it you've searched pretty thoroughly round here, de Silva?'

'Yes, sir.'

'Then we'll stand in a circle round the spot. On my signal, take forty paces out then begin.'

Solemnly, they took their stations and waited. A picture de Silva had seen of a stone circle in England that was reputed to date from the time of the Ancient Britons flashed into his mind; for a moment, he felt as if he was about to take part in some primitive pagan rite. There was something potent in the idea of circles. Maybe they would receive a sign that would lead them to the answer to the riddle of Velu's death. After all, hadn't the Buddha taught that life and death were part of one great circle?

'Shanti!' hissed Jane, glancing sideways at him. 'Do pay attention.'

'I am.'

'Really? I know that look. You were miles away. Everyone else has started walking.'

'Ah, then we must catch up.' He stepped forward briskly; he must remember that today wasn't the day for meditating on eternal truths.

It was slow going through the jungle, and the air was hot and thick, like wading through soup. Soon, sweat soaked de Silva's shirt and he could have cooked eggs under the crown of his hat. Astonishingly, Jane looked cool and composed; he attributed it to her usual calm, methodical approach to most problems.

He looked at his watch. Barely an hour had passed. A pity it wasn't time to go back and sample some of their picnic. Jane nudged him and passed the water bottle she was carrying. 'Drink some of this, dear. In this heat, it's important not to get too thirsty; far more important than going hungry.'

'You must have read my mind.'

He grinned and took a gulp from the bottle then handed it back to her. They moved on a little further. After every few steps, he investigated the ground with his stick. The memory of the unfortunate Mr Henchard sent a shiver down his spine. Snakes were sure to be close by – Ceylon had more than ninety species of them, mostly poisonous – and he had no desire to come upon one unawares. It was no use Jane telling him that a snake was likely to be more alarmed than he was. It would bite if it felt threatened. What appeared to be a mound of leaves might at any moment turn out to be a krait or a cobra. He had encountered one in a rough patch in his garden a few months previously: a magnificent creature with its mosaic of gold and black scales, but deadly poisonous. He shivered as he remembered the reptile's hooded head and baleful eyes; the long blue tongue that darted from venomous jaws.

Preoccupied with this vision of horror, he missed his footing on a mossy root and stumbled. He let out a loud yelp.

'What is it, dear?'

'My ankle!'

'You'd better sit down and let me have a look.'

He hobbled to a nearby log and slumped down. Jane knelt beside him and carefully inspected the offending ankle.

'You've grazed it badly, and I'm afraid you may have sprained it too. It feels very hot. Here, give me your handkerchief.'

She found the water bottle, soaked de Silva's handkerchief and carefully cleaned the graze, then she tied the handkerchief round his ankle as best she could and anchored it with his torn sock.

'There, that should hold it in place. I'm afraid you'll have to walk though. Perhaps it's time we started back.'

Tentatively, de Silva tested the foot.

'No, I'm alright. I don't want to be invalided out and leave my junior officers to uphold the honour of the police force.'

'Very well, but if the pain gets worse, we're going back to the car.'

They continued their wearisome progress for another hour then decided to return to the place where Velu had been found to see if the others had fared better. Clutterbuck was ahead of them, sitting on the trunk of a fallen tree, wiping his forehead with a large linen handkerchief. The stick with the silver Labrador's head lay aslant next to him. Darcy was close by in a patch of shade, his chin resting on his paws, and his tongue lolling.

'Any luck?' asked Clutterbuck.

'I'm afraid not, sir.'

'Frobisher said he'd go on a bit longer. Bags of stamina these young ones. By the time one gets to our age, it's best to know one's limitations, eh, de Silva?' He smiled at Jane. 'Although you look as if you've done nothing more strenuous than take a gentle stroll in the garden, Mrs de Silva.'

Jane laughed. 'You're very gallant.'

Looking at de Silva's torn, bulging sock, Clutterbuck frowned. 'What have you done to yourself?'

'Only a minor accident.'

'More than minor, dear,' Jane interposed. 'You scraped a lot of skin from your ankle and you've probably sprained it.'

'We don't want it getting infected,' said Clutterbuck briskly. He reached for his stick and unscrewed the finial. 'Put some of this on it.'

De Silva smelt brandy. It burned when Jane applied some to the graze and he winced. 'We have a first aid kit in the car,' she said. 'I'll fetch it.'

'We may as well all come, Mrs de Silva. It's high time we had a spot of lunch.'

Back at the cars, they were unpacking the hampers when they heard the others coming. 'Anything to report, Frobisher?' shouted Clutterbuck.

'No, sir. We all ended up at a ravine where the sides are so steep, there's no climbing down. If there's anything to be found at the bottom, I'm afraid it's going to stay hidden.'

As de Silva anticipated, Prasanna and Nadar looked askance at the sandwiches, gratefully accepting the familiar food de Silva offered.

It was the hottest part of the day and a lethargic air settled over the party. De Silva couldn't shift the fear that the expedition was a waste of time. What on earth had given him the idea that they would find anything to help the investigation out here? They didn't even know for sure what they were looking for.

'We may as well make use of the hours we have left before it gets dark,' said Clutterbuck when the meal was over. 'Do you want to stay here, de Silva?'

'No, I'll carry on.'

'I suggest we retrace out steps to that clearing where I met up with you and Mrs de Silva and go on from there.'

But it wasn't long before de Silva's ankle felt very swollen. When he pressed his fingers against the hot skin, it gave under the pressure like an overripe mango.

'I'll have to give up,' he said, wincing.

'Do you want to rest for a while before we go back to the car?' asked Jane.

He nodded and sank down on a log close by. 'I'm sorry I dragged you out on this wild goose chase,' he said glumly.

'We had to try, dear, and it's not over yet. One of the others might still find something.'

'I doubt it.'

She looked at him sympathetically. 'It's not like you to give up so easily. We can still take the pieces we have down to Colombo for a second opinion.'

'There's not much to show anyone. I don't hold out a lot of hope that they will advance the case.'

'Something's bound to come up.'

De Silva tried to rotate his ankle and flinched. 'At the moment, all that seems to be coming up is this dratted ankle.'

'Poor dear. Let's stay here for a while. Why don't you go and sit in that patch of shade over there and have a nap?' She pointed to an overhanging rock a little way off. 'That will make you feel better.'

'If you say so.'

But he had to admit, when he settled down under the overhang, the shade was very pleasant. Resting his back against the cool stone, he tipped his hat over his eyes and closed them. It was a skill he had learnt from his years in the Colombo force: the ability to catnap when an investigation entailed irregular hours and the lack of a good sleep. The sounds of the jungle lulled him into drowsiness: birds calling high up in the canopy; the crackle of leaves falling to the ground, and the patter of rain…

He pushed back his hat and looked up at the patches of sky that were visible through the trees. They were the colour of pewter.

'I think we'd better get back to the car. No point staying here for a soaking.'

Walking as fast as his ankle allowed, they set off, but after a while, Jane stopped. 'Are you sure we're going the right way? Nothing looks familiar.'

De Silva frowned. He didn't like to admit that he was lost, but she could be right, and the rain was getting heavier by the minute. Veils of mist blurred the trees. Birds that had been calling to each other or singing to warn off intruders on their territory were silent. Animals had scuttled away to find shelter; the only sound left was the steady thrum and gurgle of rain.

'Nothing to worry about,' he said firmly. 'I have everything under control.'

'I'm not sure about that, dear.'

A few steps further on, she stopped and cupped a hand to one ear. 'Did you hear that?'

'What?'

'There's someone up ahead of us.'

'Are you sure? This rain's making such a noise, I don't see how you can hear anything over it.'

'But there is someone. I'm sure of it. Over here! We're over here!'

Intently, they both listened, then she called again. This time, an answer came back.

'It's Constable Nadar!' exclaimed Jane.

A rotund figure appeared in the distance, dimly at first, then assuming the outline of the young constable. Jane waved frantically. 'Thank goodness he's found us.'

'Found us? You mean we found him. I was never lost.'

Jane gave a little snort. 'You could have fooled me, dear.'

She peered into the rain. 'Poor boy, he looks like a drowned rat, but then I don't suppose we look any better.'

Reaching them, Nadar dashed the rain out of his eyes. His raincoat flapped in the wind like a sail on the high seas, but he looked jubilant. 'We've found something, sir! Mr Clutterbuck sent me to fetch you.'

* * *

At first, de Silva saw nothing unusual about the place that Nadar led them to: the same thick tangle of rain-laden trees, their branches hung with glistening lianas, as they had been trudging through all afternoon. The soggy mulch of leaf litter under their feet gave off the same smell of decay that was everywhere in the jungle.

'Nadar! Are you certain this is right?'

'Yes, sir,' Nadar shouted back. 'Almost there.'

He dived into a particularly dense thicket of undergrowth, and, reluctantly, de Silva followed. Vegetation clawed at his trousers. When he turned to ask Jane if she needed help, her answer disappeared in the sluicing rain. The struggle seemed endless, but at last Archie Clutterbuck came into view. He stood near a pile of roughly dressed stone blocks. As de Silva came closer, he realised that they must have formed part of a building of some kind. Whatever it had been though, it was a ruin now. Trees had grown up where the roof should have been; creepers and mosses swathed what was left of the walls as if they were determined to drag everything down to oblivion.

Despite his bedraggled appearance, Archie was buoyant.

'Good show, Constable!' he boomed. 'Come and look at this, de Silva. I doubt we'd have spotted it without your chap, Prasanna. He noticed a monkey disappear into the ground, followed to see where it had gone and found some steps. There's a doorway at the bottom. Bit of a tight squeeze getting through but then... Well, you'd better come and see for yourself. You too, Mrs de Silva if you don't mind dirtying your clothes.'

'I don't think they can get in any worse state than they are now. And please don't try to say anything gallant. I'm having great fun and that's all that matters.'

Clutterbuck laughed. 'Bravo, ma'am. That's the spirit! Frobisher and Prasanna are already down there. Shall we join them?'

With Clutterbuck leading, they started off down the steps. Jane followed, picking her way carefully on the slippery stone, then de Silva, with Nadar bringing up the rear.

Blessedly, the rain was beginning to slacken. A gleam of sunshine even filtered through the dripping trees, however it took several seconds for de Silva's eyes to accustom themselves to the gloom as they descended to a doorway that looked as if it had been rather fine before tree roots and creepers did their work of destruction. Now, however, the fluted doorjambs stood aslant like drunken men and the carved lintel was cracked. Apprehensively, de Silva glanced up at the keystone; it was a foot lower than it should have been. He hoped it wasn't going to choose today to fall the rest of the way.

Ferns and other vegetation grew in the gaps between the stones. Once again, thoughts of snakes flashed into de Silva's mind; this was just the kind of dark, quiet spot they liked. He placed his feet with extra caution, watching for flickers of movement. Feeling for the truncheon on his belt, he tightened his grip. If they did disturb a representative of his least favourite reptilian species, the truncheon would be better than no weapon at all.

Clutterbuck squeezed his bulky frame through the doorway, and de Silva and the others followed. They were in a narrow passage that made it necessary to walk in single file. Shafts of sunlight coming through the fallen roof illuminated the walls. In places, words were incised in the stones, but they were too worn and encrusted with mosses to make it possible to work out what they meant.

The light grew stronger as they neared the end of the passage and emerged into a circular chamber that was open to the sky in the places where the roof had fallen in. For a moment, de Silva's eyes played a trick, and he stood aghast, as Allan Quatermain and his companions had done. He saw the monstrous figure of Death, presiding over the skeletons of men who had been rash enough to venture into the fabled King Solomon's mines. A shudder went through him, and he had to force himself to stand his ground, then the vision dissolved, and he saw that the only occupants of the chamber were Prasanna and Charlie Frobisher; both were covered in dust and cobwebs.

Hoping no one had noticed his moment of weakness, de Silva looked around him. The chamber was large enough to hold at least twenty people. Why had someone wanted to build a place of such a size in the middle of the jungle?

Charlie Frobisher straightened up and wiped the sweat from his forehead with the back of his hand. 'We've moved most of the rubble from where the roof fell in, sir,' he said, addressing Clutterbuck. He pointed to a small pile of objects. 'That's what we've found so far.'

'Anything of interest?'

'A few shards of pottery and some bones. Animal bones most likely. They may be the remains of creatures that came in here to die. Apart from that, we found a few coins like this one.'

He held out a small, dented piece of tarnished metal.

'Would you like to hazard a guess as to how old it is? You're the archaeologist among us.'

Frobisher gave a self-deprecating grin. 'I'm far from being expert, sir. My grandfather was the archaeologist in the family. As I told Inspector de Silva, he never came to Ceylon, but he had some antiquities from the region in his collection. Looking at these coins, they do resemble some of the ones he owned. If I remember rightly, he said that they were from the time of the Kandyan kings, but I'm afraid that doesn't give us a very precise date. The Kandyan kings ruled this part of Ceylon from the end of the fifteenth century up to the beginning of the nineteenth when the Kandyan kingdom became part of the British Empire.'

Clutterbuck nodded. 'It gives us a vague idea though.

How do you think the coins ended up here?'

'The Kandyan kings didn't always rule peacefully. They fought against the Portuguese and the Dutch as well as their own rebellious chiefs. This place might have been used by people trying to escape a conflict by hiding in the jungle.'

'Hmm. Interesting. If that was the case, I imagine they would certainly have brought more than a few coins and pots with them. Gentlemen, I believe we can assume that this place has been looted at some point in time. But I've yet to see evidence that it happened recently and, until I do, I'd prefer not to make assumptions that it has anything to do with the murder of this man, Velu.'

A rumble made them all look up at the places where the roof should have been. Fat, hot drops of rain quickly followed, making dark patches on the dusty ground.

'Drat!' muttered Clutterbuck. 'It looks like we're in for another wetting. Bag up the coins and the pottery, de Silva, then we'd better finish up here as fast as we can and get off. All hands to the pump. I don't mean you, Mrs de Silva,' he added hastily. 'Not a job for a lady.'

Jane's face settled into an expression de Silva knew well. 'You're very kind, but I'm perfectly capable of making myself useful,' she said firmly.

Between the six of them, they had soon looked through what remained of the wood fragments, cracked tiles and lumps of mortar lying on the ground. There were no more coins, but Jane noticed something glinting. When she bent down to retrieve it, she found that it was a small, curved piece of gold-coloured wire. She held it up to the light and they all scrutinised it.

'I wonder if it's from a piece of jewellery,' she said. 'The hook for an earring for example, or perhaps it was part of the clasp for a brooch.'

Just then, there was the noise of angry chattering. A langur monkey was perched on the splintered remains of a massive beam that would once have supported part of the roof. As it flicked its tail and bared its teeth, de Silva noticed that something in its paw caught the light. He moved closer to try to see what it was, but the creature gave a defiant screech and bounded away.

He was about to mention it to the others when there was a crash of thunder, and lightning split the sky.

'Time to go!' shouted Clutterbuck. 'We're in for a serious storm by the look of it, and it could be dangerous out here. I doubt we'll find anything else now. In any case, we can always come back.'

On the way to the cars, the heavens opened; like a monstrous beast waking from slumber, the rain crashed down.

'At least it's washed the dust off our raincoats,' said Jane as de Silva helped her into the Morris.

He closed the door then hurried round and jumped into the driver's seat. 'Whew! Cats and dogs are nothing. Today, I think it's raining elephants.'

Jane smiled. 'It certainly is. All the same, it's been worth the wetting.'

She reached into the pocket of her trousers and brought out the piece of wire she had kept. 'I wonder if it's real gold?' she mused.

De Silva shrugged. He was far more concerned with keeping the Morris on the road and trying to ignore the pain in his ankle. Visibility was rapidly diminishing with the torrential rain that had now set in. The windscreen wipers arced from one side to the other as if they were engaged in a tennis match to the death.

'What are you going to do now?' Jane asked.

'Get us home safely, I hope. I can hardly see a thing. If we come off the road, we'll be stuck here for hours. The way Archie drives, rain or no rain, he's probably halfway to Nuala by now. I doubt we can rely on him to spot us if we get into trouble.'

'I'm sure you're being too harsh, dear.'

'Well, I'd rather not find out.'

'Where are we going, by the way? Everyone was so keen to get out of the rain that we didn't agree anything.'

'I think we should go home and change into some dry clothes to start with. After that, I'll go on to the police station. Prasanna and Nadar should be there by then, and if Archie and Charlie Frobisher aren't with them, I'll telephone the Residence to discuss what we do next.'

Jane clutched the dashboard as the Morris went into a slide. His lips set in a grim line, de Silva resisted the temptation to slam his foot on the brake; with his sore ankle, it would have been a very painful thing to do in any case. Fortunately, the Morris slowed, and he was able to bring her back on course before the deep gully at the side of the road claimed its prey.

'Sorry about that. I had to swerve to miss that big stone in the middle of the road. It wasn't there on the way here. The rain must have washed it down from somewhere. I doubt the tyres would have survived a collision.'

Jane let go of the dashboard and relaxed back in her seat. 'That's quite alright, dear. As you know, I have complete faith in your driving.'

De Silva's lips twitched. 'Thank you, my love.'

'Where were we? Oh yes, what are you going to do?'

'That will depend on Archie. He obviously wasn't convinced there's a connection between Velu's murder and the building we found, but I hope I can persuade him that it's worth taking the things we found with Velu's body to Colombo for a second opinion. I don't want to take Coryat's word for it that they're worthless.'

'Don't forget the new coins and my little piece of wire.'

'I won't.'

'If Archie agrees, perhaps he'll suggest someone. Or that nice young man Charlie Frobisher may know an expert. He already has an interest in archaeology.'

'Maybe, but I was actually thinking of visiting one of my former colleagues down in Colombo.'

'Who's that?'

'You've never met him. His name's Rudi Chockalingham.'

'That's an unusual combination of names. Is he Sinhalese?'

'His father was, but his mother came from Dutch stock. He's an amusing fellow. Rather wild, and very fond of driving motorbikes extremely fast, but good at his job.'

'Which is?'

'Tracking down thieves who steal from temples and other religious buildings. Of course,' he added, 'I haven't seen him for years. He may have calmed down by now.'

'Oh, I do hope not. I'm looking forward to meeting him.'

De Silva grinned. 'So, you're determined to come?'

'After today, I'm not missing the fun.'

He reached over and patted her hand. 'Good. Rudi used to have plenty of contacts in the antiquities' world, and he knows how to be discreet. I'm sure he'll be able to find someone to give us an opinion on the pieces I showed to Coryat and today's finds without too many questions being asked.'

'You just have to persuade Archie.'

'As you say.'

Jane thought for a moment. 'I wonder if he'll want to come down to Colombo with us. He did seem very enthusiastic about today's search.' She smiled. 'At least until the rain got so heavy.'

'I don't blame him for that.'

De Silva shivered. The Morris's heater wasn't used to having to cope with so much wetness. As a result, his clothes were still damp and clammy, and he felt a tickle in his throat. He hoped his cold wasn't coming back.

'It was strange finding a building like that all on its own in the jungle,' Jane remarked after a while. 'One would need hundreds of workmen to cut all that stone and wood and make the roof tiles.'

'I expect it wasn't on its own originally. The workmen would have been given far more modest accommodation, probably wattle and mud houses with palm-frond roofs as our villagers use today. If that building's a few hundred years old, they would have collapsed and rotted away to nothing long ago.'

'I suppose you're right. It would be very interesting to know more about what went on there, and why people chose it as a place to live.'

'I expect Frobisher's right. It was a hiding place where people hoped to escape to safety during some violent period in our history. There have been many of those.'

'I wonder how long it was occupied for. I doubt anyone would go to the trouble of building from stone if they hadn't expected to stay for quite a while. It must have been someone of high status too.'

De Silva nodded. 'Which indicates that their possessions would have been valuable.'

'But would they have had time to bring them with them if they were fleeing from an enemy?'

'A good question, my love. Unfortunately, we may never know.'

* * *

Home at Sunnybank, they changed into dry clothes and one of the servants took their wet, muddy ones away to be washed. It was no wonder he'd been so cold, thought de Silva; every stitch he had on had been wet, including his underpants.

Jane removed the dressing she had applied to his ankle in the jungle. 'I'm afraid that swelling's going to take a while to go down,' she said as she applied a salve to the graze and gently rubbed it in.

'Ow! Must it be so tight?' He grimaced as she re-bandaged the ankle.

'It needs to be tight to support it. Perhaps some ice would help too.'

'I'm not sure I want any part of me getting wet again today.'

'Then rest it, at least.'

'I will later, but I must get down to the station first.'

In the drawing room, a fit of sneezing seized him. Jane clicked her tongue sympathetically. 'You'd better have some tea to warm you up before you go.'

She glanced at the clock on the mantelpiece. 'And what with sharing the picnic with Prasanna and Nadar, you didn't have much lunch. You must be hungry.'

He had forgotten the needs of his stomach in all the excitement, but with the mention of food, they reclaimed his attention. 'I am rather.'

Jane rang the bell. 'I hope Cook has something he can get ready quickly.'

'Now I come to think about food, even a sandwich sounds quite appealing.'

'It's not often I hear you say that, dear,' said Jane with a smile.

Luckily, there was some dahl and curry left from the previous evening. De Silva was soon savouring the delicious aroma of spiced sweet potatoes, cauliflower and peas. After a second helping, he felt much better.

He sat back in his chair and patted his middle. 'Just what was needed. No detective should be asked to solve a murder on an empty stomach.'

'Would you like some more tea before you go?'

'No, Nadar can make himself useful in that department. I'd better get down to the station and see what's going on.'

He raised an eyebrow. 'I notice that Archie hasn't telephoned me here. He may have had enough adventures for one day.'

'Poor Archie. At least he won't have had to face Florence's wrath for coming home in a bedraggled state.'

De Silva chuckled. 'Yes, I doubt she'd be pleased. She has such definite ideas about the dignity of Archie's position. Just as well she's safely out of the way. Now,' he pushed back his chair and stood up. 'If it's to be worth going at all, I must be off to the station. At the very least, I'd like to know what was said in Archie's car on the way back to Nuala.'

CHAPTER 12

Prasanna and Nadar were still at the station, but there was no sign of Archie or Charlie Frobisher.

'Nothing useful, sir,' said Prasanna when de Silva asked what had been discussed on the drive back to Nuala. 'Mr Clutterbuck spoke of fishing and shooting, and Mr Frobisher mostly listened.'

The British, thought de Silva irritably. And they frequently had the nerve to accuse his countrymen of being slow at getting on with whatever job needed doing. Never mind, as the two subjects were Archie's favourites, apart from golf and his dog, Darcy, it indicated that he was still in a good mood. He glanced at the clock on the wall. It was after six o'clock. As Archie hadn't telephoned or left a message, possibly it would be wise to leave calling him until morning.

Once he'd sent Prasanna and Nadar home, he spent half an hour writing notes on the day's events. Despite Archie's views, increasingly he felt convinced that the mysterious building in the jungle was connected in some way with Velu's death. The artefacts found with his body might have been a small proportion of a greater haul that had been looted.

But who had taken that haul and where was it now? Even if Clutterbuck was reluctant to query Henry Coryat's assessment of the pieces de Silva had shown him, surely, he must see that it was a mistake to give up yet. There was so much they needed to find out.

Rudi Chockalingham would know how to handle things so that word never got back to Coryat. Although the man was such a recluse that it was unlikely in any case. The only way it might happen was if today's adventure was the start of something big, and Nuala ended up being famous for a great archaeological find: a fatal one in poor Velu's case.

He locked up and climbed into the Morris. On the drive home, he amused himself with speculating whether today's expedition would go down in the history books. Howard Carter had become world famous for finding the tomb of the boy pharaoh, Tutankhamun, and so had Sir Arthur Evans for his work on the palace of Knossos in Crete. In Ceylon, the great sites at Anuradhapura and Pollonnaruwa were famous. Why shouldn't Shanti de Silva be lauded as the discoverer of – he was still trying to settle on a name when he drew up at his front door.

'I've decided that archaeology might be an interesting new string to my bow,' he said to Jane as they sat in the drawing room, enjoying their pre-dinner drinks.

She smiled. 'I do find the idea rather appealing. Let's start in Nuala, but I'd love to see Egypt one day. Do you suppose we might find something exciting there? Or Greece perhaps? With such ancient civilisations, surely there must be lots that's undiscovered. When I was a governess, I worked for a while in a family where the father was a professor of Ancient Greek. I learnt a little of the language from him, so that would be useful.'

De Silva chuckled. 'That's good, we have it all decided. Once we've finished here and we're famous, we'll take a long break from Nuala and travel the world.'

His expression turned gloomy. 'After I've got to the bottom of this murder, of course. I just hope Archie won't delay that by being in one of his stubborn moods.'

He stifled a sneeze then pulled his handkerchief out of his pocket and blew his nose. His head felt thick with catarrh.

'Oh dear, your cold must be coming back,' said Jane.

'Not surprising after the wetting today. When they come to review police pay, I hope the British will consider how I suffer in the line of duty.'

* * *

In the end, he telephoned the Residence from Sunnybank early the next morning. Archie was in a meeting, the secretary informed him, but had left a message that he would be available at eleven o'clock. De Silva spent the intervening time rehearsing what he would say, trying to anticipate Archie Clutterbuck's objections and thinking of how he would refute them.

He arrived at the Residence just before eleven and rang the bell. A servant answered and led him straight down the corridor to Clutterbuck's study. A sneeze prickled at the back of his nose as he followed the man, erupting just as he was shown in.

'Bless you!' Clutterbuck gave him a look that was almost one of sympathy. 'Nasty cold you have there. I don't suppose that weather yesterday helped.'

'I'm afraid not, sir.'

'Friar's Balsam: that's the ticket. My mother always had a bottle handy. Used to dose my brother and I up with it when we had a cold. A few drops in a bowl of steaming water, towel over the head and breathe in. Never failed to put us right.'

'Thank you. I'll remember that.'

De Silva sneezed again and blew his nose. Returning his handkerchief to his pocket he felt a wet nose brush his hand and reached down to pat Darcy. He was dry and clean now, but at close quarters, there was still a lingering smell of wet dog. 'I'm glad to see Darcy is none the worse for his outing,' he said.

'Darcy? Far from it. The old chap never minds a bit of water. Labradors are great swimmers, you know. Oh, I almost forgot. How's that ankle getting on?'

'Healing well, thank you.' He didn't want to give the impression that he was too much of an invalid.

'Glad to hear it. Right then, take a seat. Early, I know, but in the absence of Friar's, may I offer you a whisky for medicinal purposes?'

'It's most kind of you, but I won't just now.' His head was quite muzzy enough.

'Very well.' Clutterbuck sat down in his desk chair and steepled his hands. 'Now, what are your thoughts about our discovery yesterday?'

De Silva's hopes rose. This was something new; usually Archie liked to launch into his own opinions straight away.

'I appreciate we found no clear evidence that the dead man, Velu, had a connection with the place, but the coincidence is strong enough to persuade me that it's worth having the items found with his body examined for a second opinion.'

Clutterbuck picked up a pen and rotated it between his thumb and forefinger. 'I've hesitated over questioning Henry Coryat's verdict – he was, in his day, one of the most eminent men in the Museum Service.' He paused, and de Silva's optimism faltered.

'But I had plenty of time to think matters over while Darcy and I spent our solitary evening together. In the end, I came to the same conclusion that you have. With the proviso that I'd prefer it if word didn't get back to Coryat. I have no desire to offend the man.'

'That ought not to be a problem, sir.'

De Silva explained about his friend, Chockalingham, and the plan to find an expert through him.

'Excellent,' said Clutterbuck. 'If you're confident this man will be discreet, that seems a very good solution. I'll leave it with you. Keep me posted, won't you? And please give my regards to Mrs de Silva. A very sporting show she put on yesterday.' He grinned. 'I'm not sure my wife would have taken our excursion in her stride in quite the same way. Oh, and congratulate your lads for me. They did well under trying circumstances.'

De Silva smiled. 'I hope Mrs Clutterbuck is enjoying her holiday.'

'Apparently so. I had a telegram. She'll be embarking on her cruise soon. Dressing for dinner and string quartets. Dancing too, I believe. Not my line of country, I fear. Do you dance, de Silva?'

'I do, although my wife would tell you I need more practice. We acquired a gramophone for the purpose. Although sometimes I think I would do better to sit and listen to the music than try to dance to it.'

There was a whine from Darcy's direction. Clutterbuck reached down and scratched him behind the ears. 'Do you need to visit the garden, old chap?'

The elderly Labrador thumped his tail and hauled himself to his feet.

'I'll come out with you, de Silva. I expect the servants are busy, and I could do with some fresh air.'

He looked out of the window. 'Ah good, the rain's stopping. It makes a pleasant change to see a patch of blue sky. I'm not surprised my wife wanted to get away for a while. I suppose that, being born here, you're used to the monsoon. But sometimes I miss our English weather. It's a gentler creature than you have here. I never thought I'd say it, but I miss the winters too. Frost sparkling on the grass, the countryside white with snow, icicles hanging from the

91

eaves. What did Shakespeare say? Something about owls, and shepherds with freezing hands? My wife would know. She's a keen reader of Shakespeare. Yes, it's a pretty sight, a snowy winter's day. I presume you've never seen snow, de Silva?'

'I've never left Ceylon.'

'You and Mrs de Silva should take a holiday. See something of the world.'

De Silva smiled. 'She was saying the same yesterday evening. Perhaps one day we will.'

They had reached the driveway, and Darcy lolloped away in the direction of the nearest coconut palm.

'Well, I'll let you get off,' said Clutterbuck. 'Keep me up to date with how things are going and take as much time as you need down in Colombo. Why not take Mrs de Silva with you? I'm sure she'd prove an admirable sleuth. Don't stint yourselves; the Residence will pick up the tab.'

'Thank you very much, sir.'

De Silva walked over to the Morris and climbed in. Pulling away, he smiled to himself. That was one of the longest, and most affable conversations, apart from ones to do with work, that he had ever had with Archie Clutterbuck. He must have enjoyed yesterday's adventure.

CHAPTER 13

On the drive home, though, his mood altered a little. It was gratifying that Archie had come around to his way of thinking so easily, and that he had made such a generous offer of a stay in Colombo, but the suggestion that he and Jane make a holiday of it did grate a little. If the death of a Britisher had been involved, would Archie have been so relaxed?

'I think you're being oversensitive, dear,' said Jane when he grumbled about it over lunch. 'Usually, the problem is that Archie resists doing what you want him to; you should be pleased when he agrees with you without any fuss. The fact it's a villager who was murdered doesn't make it any less important. If Archie didn't take that view, he's perfectly capable of telling you not to waste police time on the case. Now, when shall we go down to Colombo? We'll need to book tickets and a hotel, but I can deal with all that if you'd like me to. It's a long time since I've been in Colombo, but I'm sure I can find a place that's not too expensive where we can be comfortable. I know you'll have work to do, but it would fun to revisit old haunts too.'

He got up and went around to her side of the table. Resting his hands on her shoulders, he kissed the top of her head. 'I'm sorry, my love; I'm being a grouch. Archie said we weren't to stint ourselves, so we'll take him at his word: book the Galle Face Hotel.'

Jane's eyes danced. 'That's the spirit! I'll have to bring my best frock.'

Leaving her to make plans, de Silva drove to the police station. The bazaar was crowded for the time of day, and he had to slow down to negotiate the mêlée of carts, shoppers, dogs, and chickens thronging the road. Above it all, the sky was now a limpid blue, although a line of dark clouds mustered on the western horizon like a herd of angry bullocks massing for a stampede. No doubt all these people hoped to complete their business before the rain came on again.

At one point, he had to wait for a handcart piled high with fruit and vegetables to lumber across in front of the Morris. A shrine to the Buddha had been set up at the corner of the crossroads. He noticed that all the candles had been doused in the last downpour. It had also turned the offerings of flowers to a soggy brown mush. Awnings over stalls steamed as they dried in the sun. In corners where its rays didn't reach, lingering puddles glinted like sheets of silver laid on the muddy ground.

Rain, rain, and more rain. Rather than go to Colombo, perhaps he should try to find an expert on antiquities in Jaffna or Trincomalee. It was the dry season there, on the other side of the island. He would never choose to live in either of those places though. The countryside around them couldn't compare with the beauty of the tea country, and, although there were some fine buildings in both cities, to his mind, Kandy far surpassed them in elegance.

Prasanna and Nadar gave the appearance of being busy when he walked into the public room at the station. He wasn't sure what they were achieving, but he gave them the benefit of the doubt. They'd worked hard yesterday in extremely unpleasant conditions.

'I'm going to trust you with a piece of information,' he said. 'But I rely on you both not to breathe a word to anyone; agreed?'

'Yes, sir,' they chorused.

'Do you recall the artefacts we found that day we discovered Velu's body?'

They nodded.

'Well, I took them to a man called Henry Coryat, an expert in the field of antiquities, and asked his opinion as to their worth. Mr Coryat considered they were virtually worthless – merely trinkets you might pick up in a bazaar any day of the week.'

Prasanna and Nadar looked downcast. 'Did you think they were valuable?' asked de Silva.

'We thought some of them might have been, sir.'

'Am I right that you felt that would make this case much more interesting than it would be if Velu was simply murdered over some village squabble?'

'Yes, sir,' said Prasanna. 'We assumed it was the reason we made the search in the jungle yesterday.'

'Then I have some good news for you. Increasingly, I've had my doubts about Mr Coryat.'

'Do you mean he was lying, sir?' asked Nadar.

'That is a possibility, or it may be that he's not as competent as he once was. Whatever the truth of the matter, Mr Clutterbuck has agreed to my getting a second opinion. Oh, by the way, he praised your hard work yesterday. Well done, both of you.'

The young men beamed.

'I'll be going down to Colombo soon to consult a man there. I'm not sure what the result will be, but this could be a turning point. Meanwhile, I'd like the two of you to scout around in the bazaar. See what information you can glean about Velu.'

He scratched his chin. 'There's the village headman's grandson too. I think I'll go back to the village this afternoon and see if there've been any developments. We can't be certain there's a connection, but any unusual circumstance needs to be followed up. If the grandson isn't back before I leave for Colombo, I rely on you, Prasanna, to keep an eye on the situation. Nadar, you can help if need be. Now, I'll be in my office. One of you put a call through to the police at Colombo for me, please.'

A few minutes later, the telephone on his desk chirruped. He picked it up and heard Nadar's voice. 'I have the police headquarters at Colombo, sir. Who shall I say you want to speak with?'

'Inspector Rudi Chockalingham.'

There was another silence then his old colleague's voice crackled down the line against a racket of typewriters and shouted conversation. Conditions at the Colombo head-quarters had clearly not improved in the years since he had been gone.

'Shanti de Silva! What a pleasure to hear from you. Are you still up in Nuala?'

'Indeed I am.'

'How's married life?'

'Excellent. The best thing I've ever done.'

'I'm glad to hear you say so. Especially as I am about to embark on the same state.'

'Tamed at last, eh?' said de Silva with a chuckle.

'My mother said it was high time.'

'Well, congratulations. Is it the end of motorbike riding?'

'That point is still to be negotiated. But tell me more about how things are with you. Are you missing the big smoke at all?'

De Silva laughed. 'There are times, but on the whole, I find quite enough excitement up here.'

'Riddles in the tea leaves? Stolen bullocks?' De Silva pictured his old colleague's mischievous grin.

'Murder this time.'

'Ah, that is a more interesting challenge. Who's the dead man?'

'A villager by the name of Velu.'

'How was he killed?'

'He was shot. The body was buried in a shallow grave in the jungle.'

'Do you think the murderer was another villager settling a score?'

'That would be a reasonable assumption if it weren't for the artefacts we found close to the body.'

'And they were?'

'Coins – old ones – and some fragments of jewellery.'

'Go on.'

'I took them to one of the British residents up here – a man called Henry Coryat who used to be a senior curator at the museum in Colombo.'

'Coryat…' Chockalingham paused. 'Ah yes, I remember the name. He retired a few years ago because of ill health.'

'He told me that nothing we'd found was valuable.'

'But I sense you weren't content to leave it there.'

'I wasn't. One of the British staff at the Residence here knows something about archaeology, and he believed there were things worth looking for in the area. I decided to investigate further.'

Chockalingham listened, dropping in an occasional comment or question, as de Silva recounted the story of the jungle adventure.

'The upshot is,' de Silva finished, 'our assistant government agent has agreed to my getting a second opinion. That's where you come in.'

There was silence at the other end of the line.

'Can you help?' prompted de Silva. 'You must know a suitable person. One who would be discreet.'

'I'm just thinking who would be best. Yes, I have an idea. Can you leave it with me for a day or two? I'll contact him and get back to you.'

'Thank you.'

'Shall I call you at the police station?'

'Or at home if you can't get me there. I have a telephone installed.'

'I'm impressed; an inspector down here doesn't qualify for one.'

De Silva gave him the number.

'Do you plan to bring the artefacts to Colombo yourself?' asked Chockalingham.

'Yes.'

'Good. We must spend an evening talking over old times. They still serve the best arrack in town at Vikram's.'

De Silva remembered the dark, smoky bar favoured by some of the Colombo force. He wondered if the ebullient Tamil who owned it had got around to cleaning up the tobacco-stained walls and ceiling since he was last there.

'I'll be glad to.'

When they had said their goodbyes, de Silva leant back in his chair and laced his hands behind his head. A good day's work: now all he had to do was wait for Rudi's call. After that, he'd report back to Archie.

He glanced at the clock on the wall. There were still a couple of hours before dusk, but if he drove out to the village to see if the headman's grandson had returned, he would probably have to drive home in the dark. He didn't relish the idea if the rain had started again, and his ankle was still painful and in need of rest. He'd leave it until morning and spend what remained of the afternoon here catching up on routine business.

CHAPTER 14

The rain came again just as he and Jane sat down to dinner. It lasted through the night, and at first, de Silva couldn't sleep. When he did manage to doze off, he dreamt that elephants were using the bungalow's roof as a dance floor. Rudi Chockalingham added to the commotion, roaring round the house on his motorbike, but when de Silva woke, he realised it was only the rain falling, and the wind buffeting the windows.

He slept again then woke a final time to find a servant placing a tray of tea on the table by the bed. The rain was over, and sunshine flooded into the room, making the silver teapot gleam.

'The memsahib sent this up for you, sahib. She is already downstairs.'

De Silva pushed a hand through his hair. 'I'll be down soon. Tell her to start breakfast without me.'

The servant poured a thin, golden stream of tea into the bone china cup. 'Very well, sahib.'

De Silva drank his tea then washed and shaved quickly. His face stared back at him from the bathroom mirror. There were traceries of lines at the corners of his eyes and on his forehead, and an increasing number of grey streaks in his hair. Age was catching up on him, but at least the drawn look he remembered from his Colombo days wasn't apparent. He had Jane and the healthier air of Nuala to thank for that.

Five years since he had left the Colombo force. Apart from a brief visit there three years ago, most of which he'd spent on the Black Lotus case in the High Court, he hadn't been back. He rinsed his razor and patted his face dry with a towel then reached for his comb. He wondered how the years had treated Rudi Chockalingham. He'd sounded on good form, but then he always was a gregarious fellow and fond of a joke.

His ankle was less painful this morning; it must have benefitted from the overnight rest. He left the bandage in place, pulled on underpants, socks, and uniform shirt and trousers then padded downstairs. He'd finish dressing after breakfast: his stomach called.

'Good morning, dear,' said Jane with a smile. 'I thought I'd let you sleep for a while. You had a restless night.'

He shrugged. 'I'm not sure why. The case is progressing according to plan for the moment.'

'How's your ankle?'

'A little better, I'm glad to say.'

'Excellent. I telephoned the Galle Face. They have rooms available this week and next.'

'Good; all we need now is a call from Rudi.'

* * *

After breakfast, he set off for the village in the jungle. As a precaution, he took a walking stick with him. Even though his ankle had improved, he had quite a long walk in prospect.

Driving through town, the gullies on either side of the road still ran with water from the overnight rain. Out in the countryside, coils of mist drifted among the trees. When he reached the dirt road, the surface was slippery with mud. Parking the Morris close to where the road dwindled into a mere track leading into the jungle, he changed his shoes for the stout boots he had taken the precaution of bringing with him and set off.

Now he was alone, the walk seemed more intimidating than it had when he came this way with Prasanna. The deeper he penetrated, the more malevolent the squawks and whistles of hidden birds sounded. The track widened a little and he saw that this was because on either side, saplings had been wrenched from the ground and branches ripped from the taller trees. Giant feet had churned up the earth. Elephants had passed this way; perhaps not long ago. In addition, the improvement in his ankle soon wore off. He was glad he had brought the walking stick and did his best to use it to keep his weight on his good foot.

At a fork, he hesitated then took the left side. It wasn't long, however, before he doubted he had made the right choice. He stopped, wondering whether he should go back then decided to walk a little further on in the hope of recognising a landmark. He vaguely remembered seeing a fine banyan tree whose aerial roots had grown into thick trunks, encircling their host tree.

A few more minutes of walking and, to his relief, the banyan came into view. He found a log and sat down to rest, gazing at the massive tree. It was hard to believe that all this had grown from a tiny seed. It must be ancient, at least by the standards of the jungle where everything grew so quickly. There was something cathedral-like about the lofty arcade formed by the aerial roots that had swept down from the crown of the parent tree to plant themselves in the rich red earth. The parent tree's hollow trunk was very thin in places, crisscrossed with parasitic vines. In a few years, it would rely entirely on its progeny to stay upright.

His musings were interrupted by a loud crack close by. His heartbeat quickened: elephants? Perhaps he should take refuge behind one of the banyan's roots. So long as the creatures didn't see him, or did, but with their weak eyesight thought he was part of the tree, they shouldn't be alarmed and attack. Jungle lore claimed that elephants heard better through their feet than they did with their ears, detecting shaking of the ground inaudible to humans. Cautiously, he moved to the nearest giant root and slipped into its shadow.

Time passed, and nothing happened. De Silva's heartbeat returned to its usual rate. He was about to carry on when there was a commotion that set his heart racing once more. Out of the trees shot a jungle fowl, flying low. Fleetingly, de Silva thought he saw a brown face watching him from a break in the wall of green, then it was gone.

The fowl settled on the ground, its scarlet wattle still quivering with indignation, then recovered and started to peck for grubs in the leaf litter. De Silva noticed that some of its cobalt-blue tail feathers were missing. He wondered how it had happened. The bird didn't seem to be moulting otherwise. Perhaps the face he'd seen was that of a villager who'd decided to come out into the jungle to hunt for the pot.

At last he reached the village. The first thing he noticed was that there was some damage to the village well, presumably caused by the heavy rain. Part of the side had collapsed, and a party of men was shovelling earth out of the hole and repositioning stones.

The headman leant on his stick directing operations. When he saw de Silva, he came over and greeted him with grudging civility.

'Problems with the well?' de Silva asked.

'Always problems when the monsoon comes. What can I do for you, Inspector?'

'Has your grandson returned?'

A shake of the head. The headman jabbed his stick at the diggers and the pile of earth they had removed from the hole. 'His mother still wails,' he said grimly. 'Maybe I tell them to bury her under that.'

What a charmer, thought de Silva. 'Are any of the other young men missing today?'

A wary look came into the headman's eyes. 'Has there been more trouble? I am not responsible for all of them.'

De Silva refrained from pointing out that, technically, he was.

'I thought I saw a young man hunting jungle fowl on the way here. Why isn't he here helping?'

The headman hobbled over to the group working at the well, spoke to them briefly then came back. 'They say no one went out hunting this morning.'

'Are they sure?'

'Yes, sahib.'

The headman looked nettled, and de Silva sighed inwardly. Probably someone had, but how would he prove it? In any case, it was probably a harmless expedition. The British didn't make a fuss about villagers hunting for the pot, only when they tracked and hunted big game without the proper licence. If Clutterbuck was right about the headman having a good reputation with the British though, de Silva wasn't sure why he felt the need to be defensive. Maybe his reputation was undeserved. Still, he wasn't the quarry today; no point going off on a tangent from the purpose of the visit.

'Very well, if you're certain.'

He looked over at the well. 'Your men would get on faster if there were fewer of them working at the same time. So many feet stepping on the ground around the well weakens the soil and makes it fall back in. I suggest you organise them into smaller groups. The next time rain comes, you will find you have only made the problem worse.'

A muttered reply that de Silva didn't choose to catch came from the headman.

'I'll leave you to it,' he called out breezily, as he walked away. It was always good to have the last word.

At the banyan tree, whoever had been watching him from the trees was nowhere in sight. The jungle fowl was still there but it skittered away at his approach. The bird had been lucky; a pity he hadn't. It might be worth another call to Inspector Singh at Hatton. If nothing new came from that, maybe he'd have to abandon the grandson as a line of inquiry.

CHAPTER 15

The call from Rudi Chockalingham came the next day. The man he had in mind, a senior curator at the Colombo museum, was willing to meet with de Silva and look at the artefacts.

'I'm afraid I let slip that they had already been appraised by another expert though,' he said. 'He was surprised you couldn't find anyone closer to Nuala. But he assured me his lips would be sealed.'

De Silva sighed inwardly. A pity, but there was no help for it now.

'Did you tell him it was Coryat?'

'No, I told him the name was confidential, and he accepted that.'

'Good. Thank you for making the arrangements. When can I meet him?'

'The museum offices will be closed over the weekend, but he agreed to early next week. Just telephone me to say when you'll arrive in Colombo, and I'll confirm a time with him.'

'Excellent.'

'The curator's name is Professor Mahindra Jayakody, by the way. Let me know how it goes when we have that arrack, eh?'

There was a touch of contrition in Rudi Chockalingham's voice. De Silva thanked him once again, more warmly this time. Anyone could make a mistake.

* * *

'That's perfect,' said Jane. 'I won't need to let the vicar's wife down. I promised to help at church on Sunday. We can take the train to Kandy on Monday and change to the sleeper for Colombo. We'll have the Tuesday morning to drive to the hotel and settle in. You can see this Professor Jayakody in the afternoon if he's still free. After that, we can enjoy our little holiday.'

De Silva laughed. 'I'll let Rudi know. I'm glad you have it all worked out, my love.'

'Oh, I do. I must check what time we need to be on board the sleeper. If we're lucky, and your ankle's up to it, there might be a chance to take a walk in the Botanical Gardens at Peradeniya beforehand. It's so long since we've been there. I'd love to visit it again.'

'I'd like that too.'

'Are you going back to work this afternoon?'

'I'd better for a few hours. I don't want Prasanna and Nadar getting too much into the habit of slacking.'

'I'll book the hotel and send one of the servants for the rail tickets while you're gone.'

She beamed. 'What a treat this will be.'

'Even more so if it turns up something useful for the case.'

'Whatever happens, at least no one can accuse you of leaving any stones unturned.'

CHAPTER 16

On the Monday, a servant drove them to the train station at Nanu Oya where they boarded the train for Kandy. De Silva was relieved to find that his ankle was giving him very little pain, and his cold had almost gone.

The journey was uneventful. He spent the time reading, occasionally looking out of the window to see the green hills give way to the lowland landscape. Dense plantations of rubber and banana trees testified to the richness of the soil. From time to time, their dark green was interrupted by shimmering expanses of rice fields brimming with monsoon rain. Small villages raced by; children waved excitedly; brightly coloured prayer flags fluttered on trackside shrines; small lakes glittered, and egrets rose in white clouds from the fields.

'We're lucky to have a dry day for the journey,' said Jane. 'It should be beautiful in the Botanical Gardens.'

De Silva craned his neck. 'Look over there, there are grey clouds coming in.'

'I'm sure the rain will hold off until we're safely on the sleeper.'

'If you say so, my dear.'

The plump gentleman who was the only other occupant of the First Class carriage looked up from his copy of the *Kandy Times*. 'I agree with you, ma'am,' he said. 'The forecast in the paper is for dry weather until late tonight.'

Jane smiled at him. 'Thank you, sir.'

The plump man folded his newspaper and smoothed the creases with well-manicured fingers. An expensively tailored, cream three-piece suit; a bow tie that matched his shiny, dark-brown shoes, and a hat made of fine straw gave him a dapper air. He looked to be a man at ease with the world.

'My name is Joseph Edelman,' he said. 'May I take the liberty of asking yours?'

'I'm Jane de Silva, and this is my husband, Shanti.'

'Are you travelling all the way to Kandy?'

'Yes, we are.'

'Ah, I'm delighted to hear it. Train journeys without good company are tedious. I've travelled this line many times. Lovely as the scenery is, it pales after a while.'

He placed the newspaper on the seat beside him and tapped one of the articles. 'I'm afraid there is still no news of Miss Earhart. I doubt there's any hope of finding her now.'

The aviatrix, Amelia Earhart, had taken off from New Guinea at the beginning of the month, heading for Howland Island, a speck of land two thousand miles away in the vastness of the Pacific Ocean. Her aim was to be the first woman to pilot an aeroplane round the world. Eight hundred miles into the flight, the coastguard vessel with which she was in radio contact lost track of her. Since then, no trace of her plane had been found.

'What a tragic loss,' said Jane sadly. 'It was such a courageous plan.'

'Indeed; Miss Earhart is, or I fear we must say was, a brave lady. I have never travelled by air myself, and I don't think I should like to. I prefer to go by train.' He smiled. 'As I expect you have realised, I'm not British; I am from Switzerland. We have lakes and mountains, but no ocean bordering our country. The idea of nothing but water and sky as far as the eye can see alarms me.'

'What brings you to Ceylon?' de Silva asked.

'My business. I deal in precious stones. Ceylon is renowned for the quality of its rubies and sapphires. After I concluded my transactions in Colombo, I decided to enjoy a few days in the hills. Now it's time for me to return to Colombo. I have a passage booked on a ship that sails for Europe next week.'

They chatted amicably until the journey ended, then, wishing the amiable Swiss goodbye, went to arrange for their luggage to be kept safe at the station until it was time to board the sleeper.

Hiring a rickshaw for the short journey to the gardens at Peradeniya, they soon arrived and strolled in.

The first impression a visitor has on entering the gardens is of vibrant colour. Flowerbeds overflowing with a profusion of flowers pepper the sweeping emerald green lawns. Then the eye takes in meandering paths that draw one further in. Magnificent trees offer shade; the lazy course of the Mahweli River widens to a lake carpeted with waterlilies, and sweet, spicy scents fill the air.

Much as de Silva loved flowers, it was the trees in the gardens that impressed him most: the gigantic Java fig tree that spread like a huge living umbrella, taking up most of its surrounding lawn; the stately avenue of royal palms, and a towering tree planted as a sapling by the then British Prince of Wales, when he made his state visit to Ceylon in the previous century.

When he was a child, de Silva had been fascinated by the cannonball tree close by. The melon-sized seed pods that gave the tree its name sprouted straight from the trunk, interlaced with long, knobbly stems that carried deep pink flowers, the shape of which reminded him of giant slugs.

'My parents brought me here sometimes when I was a child,' he said. 'My mother had relations in Kandy we visited occasionally. I liked it when one of the pods fell from the tree and exploded on the ground. The stench was terrible though.'

He looked at his watch. 'It's later than I thought. We'll have to walk a bit faster if we're to see everything.'

'Are you sure you can manage?'

'Definitely. My ankle's fine now.'

Quickening their pace, they found the out-of-the-way corner of the garden where the famous colony of fruit bats nested in the trees, making the branches restless with their constant comings and goings. Lastly, they went to the orchid house.

'How beautiful they are,' said Jane, smelling a pale-yellow flower with burgundy markings at its throat. 'Especially the scented varieties.' She frowned. 'Shanti? Is something wrong?'

With a start, he looked up. 'Sorry, I was thinking about the case.'

'You're not regretting we've come, are you?'

'No, but I wonder if I did the right thing confiding in Rudi Chockalingham. There might have been other ways of finding an expert to give a second opinion.'

'Oh, I don't expect it will matter. Henry Coryat's been gone from the museum for a long time. This man probably wouldn't even know him. Anyway, you don't have to give his name.'

De Silva shrugged. 'That's true. All the same, I would feel better if Rudi hadn't slipped up.'

They reached the gates and looked around in vain for a rickshaw.

'How tiresome,' said Jane. 'I'm sure there were dozens free on the way in.'

'Always the same when one's in a hurry. We should have left sooner.'

A voice called out to them and they looked up to see their companion from the train leaning out of the window of a car. 'If you're bound for Kandy station, may I offer you a lift?' he asked with a smile.

'Why thank you,' said Jane. 'We hadn't expected it to be so busy here at this time of day.'

Edelman motioned to the man who sat in the passenger seat next to the driver. The man, who de Silva guessed was Edelman's servant, jumped out and held the door to the back seat open for them to get in.

'Thank you again,' said Jane. 'I was beginning to be afraid we'd be late.'

'It's my pleasure. Did you enjoy your walk?'

'Very much.'

'Alas, I had a business appointment – that is why I arranged to have a car at my disposal – otherwise I would have liked some exercise myself.'

Soon, they reached the station. The de Silvas thanked Edelman for his help then collected their luggage and paid a porter to take it to the train.

'I'd forgotten how crowded Kandy is,' said Jane as they followed the porter down the platform. Trolleys piled with luggage rumbled along; passengers for Second and Third Class carried boxes and bundles on their heads; food vendors' stalls did a brisk trade, and beggars held out pleading hands. 'I expect Colombo will be even more of a shock,' she added.

'We've become country pumpkins in the years we've been away, my love.'

She giggled. 'Bumpkins, dear.'

But, in the hubbub, he didn't hear her. He felt a headache coming on and his cold seemed to be getting worse again. Perhaps he had done a bit too much today. He hoped Jane would agree to have an early dinner and read until bedtime.

With relief, he saw they had reached their carriage. He checked that the porter stowed their luggage in the right place and tipped him. Jane was already in their compartment when he boarded the train.

'You look tired, dear.'

'I am rather, and this wretched cold won't go away. If you don't mind, I'd like to eat early and come back here.'

'If we finish dinner too soon, the attendant may not have come to get the bunks ready, but I suppose we can ask if we see someone.'

'Oh, I'm perfectly content to read in our seats for a while. They can do the bunks later.'

'Very well.'

At least, de Silva thought, I will be content if I manage to give my head a rest from puzzling over this case.

CHAPTER 17

Polished mahogany panelling lined the walls of the First Class dining car. Brass fittings gleamed in the glow cast by bracket lamps with bell-shaped shades of etched glass. Crisp white cloths covered the tables; the cutlery was silver, and the crockery marked with the badge of the Royal Ceylon Railways, a picture of a stupa and an elephant, in a terracotta, brown and gold roundel surmounted by the Imperial crown.

As he and Jane settled at their table, de Silva admired the scene. What a pity the menu was less likely to impress him. A steward hurried over and shook out their napkins with a ceremonial flourish then placed them in their laps. Menus printed on thick cream card were brought.

'Hmm. Tomato soup; fishcakes; lamb cutlets with Duchesse potatoes and petits pois, or vegetable curry; Queen of Puddings; cheese; coffee.'

Jane gave him an admonishing look. 'I'm sure it will be delicious, dear.'

'I hope so.'

'Why don't you have a whisky and soda first? That will make you feel better.'

'I might just do that.'

'Good evening!'

A jovial voice interrupted their conversation. De Silva looked up to find Joseph Edelman beaming down at him.

'I see I'm not alone in preferring to dine early. Late meals are so bad for the digestion.' He patted his ample stomach with a podgy hand. The signet ring on his little finger caught the light. 'And with a constitution as delicate as mine, one cannot be too careful.'

'Do join us, Mr Edelman,' said Jane with a bright smile.

'It would be a great pleasure, but I hesitate to intrude.'

'Not at all. Shanti and I will be delighted to have your company, won't we, Shanti?'

De Silva forced a smile. The Swiss was a genial fellow and under other circumstances, he would have been only too happy to share a table with him. Tonight, however, as he wasn't feeling at his best, he had hoped to eat in peace and not linger over the meal. 'Of course,' he said, concealing his reservations.

A steward appeared and set another place. Edelman studied the menu briefly then they ordered – cutlets for Jane and Edelman, the curry for de Silva. As Jane had suggested, he also asked for a whisky and soda.

'They have a very tolerable wine list here,' said Edelman. 'I think I will choose something tonight. It will help me to sleep. Mrs de Silva, can I persuade you to have a glass with me? A little thank you for letting me share your table.'

Jane hesitated. 'I don't usually indulge, but thank you, that would be very nice.'

'Mr de Silva?'

'It's kind of you to offer, but whisky is more to my taste.'

'I imagine you find English food rather bland,' remarked Edelman when the steward had gone. 'Luckily for me, it is not so very different from what you would find in my country. We Swiss do not eat very spicy food. We are very fond of cheese, however. Swiss cheese is among the most delicious in the world.'

The whisky and wine arrived, shortly followed by the soup. It was a dull shade of red and had a metallic taste. Any resemblance to tomatoes was hard to detect. The fishcakes were little better and, as the effects of the whisky wore off, he felt himself going downhill. He ate only a few mouthfuls of the curry before deciding to make his excuses and return to the compartment.

'Poor you,' said Jane. 'I do hope you won't think us rude, Mr Edelman. My husband really has been very unwell with this dreadful cold.'

De Silva blew his nose. 'There's no need for you to come, my love. You must stay and finish your dinner. I'm sure our friend here would be happy to see you safely back to our compartment.'

'Of course,' said Edelman. 'But would it not be wise to stay a while? If one has been unwell, one needs plenty of food to keep up the strength. Perhaps another whisky will help.' He beckoned to the steward hovering nearby.

De Silva shook his head. 'No, thank you. I really would prefer to get some rest.'

'Mrs de Silva, I appeal to you: help me to convince your husband.'

Edelman's tone was conventionally polite and his expression one of friendly concern, but de Silva's antennae prickled. Edelman had put down his red wine. Moisture glistened on the outside of the glass where his palm had been.

With a smile, de Silva stood up. 'Forgive me, sir. I hope to be better company at breakfast.'

Turning, he made his way to the end of the dining car, half expecting Edelman to follow, then chided himself for being too imaginative. Edelman was probably just feeling the heat. He had imbibed several glasses of Burgundy, and the meal was a heavy one too.

He reached his and Jane's compartment and put a hand on the door then froze. Someone was moving about inside. They hadn't seen an attendant to ask for their beds to be made up early. In any case, an attendant would be unlikely to close the door. Intently, he listened again. There was a snap, as if a lock was being opened, followed by a thud and a muttered curse.

He flung the door open and the figure in the compartment swung round. He was taller than average and dressed in the ubiquitous white tunic and trousers of the sub-continent. A scarf wound around the lower half of his face made it impossible to see clearly what he looked like.

Jane's suitcase was on the floor, the lock smashed, and her clothes scattered. The intruder dropped the valise he was holding. De Silva noticed a slash in the leather. He stretched out his arms to block the doorway.

'You're under arrest. Stay exactly where you are.'

A look of horror came into the intruder's dark eyes. His attack caught de Silva off guard. He gasped as a fist connected with his solar plexus. Stumbling, he lunged for the man's collar and felt the material rip. A punch to the jaw sent him reeling. The back of his head slammed into the window opposite the compartment door, and fireworks exploded in front of his eyes. It took him a moment to recover then he staggered after the intruder.

There was shouting now and the sound of pounding feet. A hand gripped his elbow, and someone pushed past him. The intruder was still in front when they reached the Second Class section of the train, but the man ahead of de Silva was gaining ground. He was dimly aware of a blur of faces as passengers broke off talking or woke from their dozes to eye the commotion with curiosity or indifference.

In the first of the Third Class carriages, the intruder jumped over a pile of bundles and boxes left in the aisle and kept running. Less agile, his pursuer had to slacken his pace to push past. As he did so, de Silva saw with a jolt of surprise that it was Joseph Edelman. He was amazed that the little Swiss could put on such a turn of speed.

They were in the final carriage now. Loud noises behind de Silva made him glance over his shoulder. Shouting guards and attendants had joined in the chase. A rush of air hit him as he turned the corner at the end of the carriage. The door crashed against the side of the train. The intruder's fingers clawed at the jamb while blurred shapes unrolled in the darkness behind him like a reel of film. Edelman took a step towards him. He seemed to be reasoning with him, but the words were lost in the roar of the train.

A blast of soot whirled past, shrouding the intruder's head. A yell that curdled de Silva's blood came out of the cloud then died, leaving only the rush of wind and the thrum of wheels. Then the screech of the train's brakes drowned them both.

* * *

'Poor fellow. I wish I could have saved him,' said Edelman mournfully.

He looked down at the mangled corpse laid out beside the line. 'To lose one's life for the sake of a few trinkets. It's a terrible indictment on the state of the world.'

There had been a good deal of shunting once the train ground to a halt. De Silva and Edelman, accompanied by the chief guard and a few of his men, had supervised the grisly process of extracting the intruder's body from where it was trapped under the train. The head was crushed beyond recognition and one arm torn off. The dead man's lifeblood soaked his tunic and trousers.

'Shortly before I saw you fighting with him, Mr de Silva, I discovered that he had already visited my compartment. Fortunately, I wasn't travelling with anything of value. The jewels I purchased here are all safely locked up in the vaults of a reputable bank in Colombo, awaiting collection before

I sail for Europe. I hope you lost nothing of importance, sir?'

De Silva thought quickly. 'No. My wife was wearing her jewellery, and I hadn't left any money in the compartment.'

The head guard poked gingerly at the dead man's clothing. 'There seems to be nothing concealed about his person, gentlemen. But if you do find anything has been taken, I'll arrange a search of this section of track when it's daylight.'

'I doubt that will be necessary,' said Edelman. 'Would you agree, Mr de Silva?'

'I would.'

He did his best to sound composed, but de Silva's mind raced. If the man had managed to find any of the artefacts he was taking to the museum, he certainly didn't want anyone else collecting them up. If anything was missing, he'd have to think of a way round the problem.

'I may as well check my luggage now,' he said, feigning calm. 'Then we'll know the situation. I don't want to hold up the train unless it's absolutely necessary.'

'Thank you, sir.'

'I'll do the same,' Edelman said.

Jane hurried towards them as they walked back along the track. 'Shanti! Are you alright?'

'Perfectly.'

'But your face! It's swollen and there's a terrible bruise coming up.'

'Oh, it's nothing.'

Jane took his arm. 'I don't think so. If there's a doctor on board, I want him to have a look at you.'

His smile twisted into a grimace of pain. 'If you insist. But after I've made sure nothing was taken.'

'You're very wise, Mrs de Silva,' said Edelman. 'Your husband took some very nasty blows. I'm glad I was close by to help him chase the intruder. Who knows what might have happened otherwise?'

'Incidentally, why did you come back, Herr Edelman?' asked de Silva. 'I'm most grateful you did, of course,' he added hastily.

'Pure fluke, sir. Your wife was asking about my family. I always carry a few photographs of them. She said she would like to see them, so I came to collect the envelope I carry them in while we waited for the dessert to be served. I was just in time to see you fall and this wretched fellow take flight.'

They had reached the First Class section of the train. De Silva put his hand on the grab rail and pulled himself up the high steps, suddenly aware that more of him than his face was bruised. He limped to his compartment, aware that the ache in his ankle had returned. Glancing over his shoulder to ascertain that no one had followed him, he grabbed the valise where he had stowed the artefacts. The lock was intact but, to make sure, he pulled the key out of his pocket and opened it. Everything was as it should be. He breathed more easily.

Footsteps approached and there was a knock at the door. Quickly, he snapped the lock shut and hoisted the valise back into the overhead locker. The effort made his ribs feel as if they were on fire. It was the chief guard who came in. 'All in order, sir?'

'Yes, thank you. I must have disturbed this would-be thief before he had time to get very far.'

'Clearly the thief broke into my compartment first.' The sound of Edelman's heavily accented voice came from the corridor, followed by the little Swiss in person. 'I'm confident, however, that nothing valuable was taken. I suggest we proceed on our journey and put this distressing interlude behind us. I propose to return to the dining car. After all the excitement, a glass of cognac would be very welcome. I hope you and your husband will join me, Mrs de Silva.'

'But what about your compartment?' asked Jane. 'Can we help you put it to rights?'

'Ach, there's no need. My servant will repack my belongings later.'

'Shall I send to find him now, sir?' asked the chief guard.

'No, not yet; I want to supervise him while he carries out the task. But after I've had my cognac.'

He turned to Jane and Shanti and smiled. 'Shall we go?'

* * *

'Poor Mr Edelman,' Jane said as they got ready for bed later. 'I think the incident shook him up more than he cared to admit. I wish he had let us help him.'

'Sometimes it's best to leave people to do things in their own way.'

'I suppose so. After all, we are virtually strangers.' She sat down at the little table by the window, unpinned her hair and started to brush it. 'You look very preoccupied, Shanti. What are thinking about?'

'Wondering if it was purely chance that the thief chose this train.'

'You mean he had a tip off we were taking things to the museum?'

'Perhaps.'

'But who would have let it slip? Apart from ourselves, only Archie, your friend Rudi, and the curator he's recommended know anything about this. How would it benefit any of them to arrange to have the things stolen?'

'I agree it seems unlikely.'

'Anyway, ours wasn't the only compartment involved.'

'True.'

'I think you should stop worrying and try to get some sleep. I hope the arnica's making your face less painful. I wish we'd found a doctor. It was all I had with me.'

'It's doing an excellent job.'

He climbed the ladder to his bunk and settled himself

under the sheet. 'In any case, after the evening I've had, and a glass of cognac into the bargain, I shall probably sleep like a baby.'

Closing his eyes, he listened to the muted clickety-clack of the train. The sound was very soothing. Firmly, he banished the spectre of the disfigured corpse by the line. Soon, he was asleep.

CHAPTER 18

What was left of the night was uneventful. De Silva woke feeling surprisingly refreshed, then confused. Where was he? Rolling over, he accidentally pressed on his cheek and let out a shout of pain. Immediately, the happenings of the previous night flooded back.

'Shanti! What's wrong?' His shout had woken Jane.

He rubbed his chin with tentative fingers. 'My face hurts.'

'I should think it does. You'll have to take care for a week or two.'

With a groan, he shifted himself to the ladder and climbed down. The mirror above the wash basin revealed a piteous sight.

'I look as if I've gone five rounds with Joe Louis,' he muttered glumly. He put a forefinger in his mouth and explored his teeth. 'At least he didn't loosen any of these.'

Jane looked at him sympathetically. 'It doesn't look that bad.'

'Oh, I think it does. I'll frighten small children in the street.'

She laughed. 'We can always buy you a mask to wear and pretend it's for a festival.'

'Very humorous.'

'Would you like me to ask the attendant to serve our breakfast in here?'

'No, I have to face the world sometime. It may as well be now.'

He tweaked back one corner of the curtain. 'We're in a siding. I suppose we're having to wait for a platform to be free.' He looked at his watch. 'The train's not due in for another hour or so anyway.'

The dining car was quiet which suited de Silva admirably. He was glad not to have to withstand the curiosity of too many other passengers. He was making a cautious attempt to eat a plate of scrambled eggs while moving his jaw as little as possible when a concerned voice addressed them. He didn't need to look up; he recognised the accent straight away.

'I fear you bear the scars of battle, Mr de Silva.'

Rather to de Silva's annoyance, Edelman's rosy cheeks and bright eyes testified to a full recovery from the previous night's disturbance.

'But we're very glad to see you looking unscathed, Mr Edelman, aren't we, Shanti?'

De Silva made a sound that could be interpreted either way, then felt churlish. In hindsight, he wished that the Swiss hadn't got involved. Had he been able to get close to the intruder himself, he might have been able to stop him jumping and had a chance to question him. In the circumstances, however, it wasn't fair to blame Edelman for acting decisively.

'I breakfasted early,' he went on. 'I slept much better than I expected. Order is restored to my luggage, and I plan to spend a few peaceful days in town before it's time to board the ship. It's been a great pleasure making your acquaintance. Perhaps we'll meet again one day.'

He lifted Jane's hand to his lips and kissed it. 'I wish you every happiness, my dear Mrs de Silva. If you find yourself in Zurich, it would be an honour to entertain you. My shop is in the Bahnhofstrasse; anyone will tell you where that is.'

He held out his hand to de Silva. 'And my good wishes to you too, sir. I hope recovery is swift.'

'What a delightful man,' whispered Jane as Edelman walked away. 'I wonder if we'll see him again. He didn't mention where he was staying.'

De Silva forked up the last of his scrambled egg and waved away the steward offering toast. 'Maybe he has friends in Colombo. We'll have to catch up with him in Zurich one day. Perhaps we'll take a cruise like Florence.'

'Switzerland has no coastline, dear.'

'I know that. I was testing you.'

She raised an eyebrow. 'You must be feeling better.'

A jolt made the tea in de Silva's cup ebb and flow like the tide. The train moved forward a few feet.

Jane peered out of the window. 'There's a man out there waving a green flag. If you've eaten enough breakfast, we ought to go and get ready.'

Wistfully, de Silva looked at a passenger on another table who was polishing off a hearty plateful of fried food. Breakfast was one of the few things he found appetising about British cooking.

'I'm coming,' he said resignedly.

CHAPTER 19

The station at Colombo was even more crowded than the one at Kandy and the vendors even more persistent. Once de Silva and Jane had extricated themselves and made sure their luggage was following with a porter, they went out to the concourse and hired a rickshaw to take them to the Galle Face Hotel. Waiting for the luggage to be loaded, de Silva noticed a sleek black car where a uniformed chauffeur held open the door for Joseph Edelman to climb in. The door closed, and the chauffeur hurried round to the driver's side. The car drew away, weaving through the throng of pedestrians, rickshaws and luggage carts.

'What is it, dear?' asked Jane.

'Oh, nothing. I just saw your friend, Mr Edelman, getting into a very expensive chauffeured Daimler. I must say, he seems to have life well organised. There must be plenty of money in the jewellery trade.'

He hauled himself awkwardly into the back seat of the rickshaw.

'Still painful?' asked Jane with a frown. 'Perhaps we can find a doctor here in Colombo.'

'Nonsense. It's only a bit of bruising, and I have work to do.'

They were soon in sight of their destination. As the rickshaw jolted down The Strand, to their right the vast expanse of the palm-fringed Indian Ocean stretched away to the horizon. The hotel's white walls gleamed in the sunshine. The building could have been a maharajah's palace, its imposing façade bookended by projecting wings, with a huge porte cochère in the middle section where cars and rickshaws bringing in hotel guests were drawing up.

De Silva paid off the rickshaw man, and a doorman dressed in a white suit with gold buttons and white gloves greeted them. They were shown to their room on the first floor.

Jane clapped her hands. 'Oh, it's lovely! Look at the view, Shanti! Isn't it wonderful to be able to see the ocean?'

Lightly, she stroked the curtains. The material rippled like water. 'And look at these – made of this beautiful golden silk, and the same for the bedspread. And these flowers' – she touched one of the petals of an arrangement of cream lilies and roses that filled the room with their perfume. 'Are you sure Archie won't complain about the cost?'

'He'd better not; he told me to spoil you.'

'How sweet of him.'

He looked at his watch. 'We have a few hours until lunchtime. I suppose I should go to the police station and let Rudi know I've arrived. Do you mind?'

'You go. I'll be perfectly happy here. Do you want to change into your uniform?'

'Not for the moment; I'd rather be anonymous.' He patted his pocket. 'But I have my badge in case I need it. I'll come back as soon as possible. We'll have a spot of lunch and then a stroll beside the ocean. Apparently, this man Jayakody won't be free until late afternoon, so we should have plenty of time.'

Leaving Jane to unpack and explore the hotel, de Silva went down to the lobby and ordered a rickshaw. Memories of his Colombo days flooded back as he travelled through the familiar city.

He'd always thought Colombo owed much of its charm

to the contrast between the elegance of the colonial buildings and the colourful variety of daily life going on in the streets. Every kind of conveyance was there: motor cars, rickshaws, bicycles, bullock carts, and even a few elephants. Horns hooted; bells rang; whips cracked; dogs barked, and cart wheels rumbled. Men sat astride the water carts that trundled along spraying water from hoses fitted at the back to keep down the dust.

Children darted about, narrowly avoiding being run over. Here and there, men lounged in the shade of the trees, smoking or playing dice or cards. Others trudged along, burdened by the goods balanced on their heads. The vivid colours of women's saris flashed through the crowds like tropical fish in a reef. Buddhist monks in orange robes walked with heads bowed as if oblivious to the cacophony surrounding them.

By the time he reached the police station, de Silva felt exhilarated by the liveliness of his old city. He showed his badge to the guard on the door and went in. At the public counter, he gave his name and asked to see Rudi Chockalingham.

The sergeant in charge gave him a strange look. 'What's your business with Inspector Chockalingham?'

'Confidential.' De Silva flashed his badge again. 'Now just tell him I'm here, will you?'

'I'm sorry, Inspector, I can't do that.'

De Silva frowned. Why did he always have to get the idiot?

'Why not?'

'Because he's not at the station today.'

'I'll leave a message then. When will he be back?'

The sergeant's brow furrowed; he seemed to be thinking deeply. 'Hard to say,' he volunteered at last.

Exasperation welled in de Silva's chest. 'You must have some idea,' he said, trying to contain it.

'Is there a problem, Sergeant?'

The man who spoke had just come through the swing doors leading from the main offices. He wore the uniform of a chief inspector and sported a handlebar moustache. He looked to be about de Silva's age.

'This officer wants to see Inspector Chockalingham, sir. Says he has confidential business with him.'

A frown flitted across the chief inspector's face. 'I'll handle this, Sergeant.'

He turned to de Silva. 'We'd better go to my office.'

Apprehensively, de Silva followed him back through the swing doors. He hadn't intended to speak to anyone but Rudi, but he needed to know what had happened to him. He'd have to be careful to divulge as little as possible.

The office they went into was large and light. Several framed photographs of Rudi's colleague being presented with awards hung on the walls. One showed him shaking hands with a man de Silva recognised as the Governor General. The bookshelves contained an impressive array of leather-bound legal and police procedural volumes.

'Please take a seat.' The man gestured to the mahogany chair on one side of the desk then sat down opposite. 'I'm Chief Inspector Fonseka,' he said.

'Inspector Shanti de Silva, now of the Nuala police force, but formerly stationed down here. I spoke with Inspector Chockalingham a few days ago and arranged to meet him.'

'Ah, Inspector de Silva. I feared it might be you. I'm afraid I have bad news.'

CHAPTER 20

A chill came over de Silva. Fonseka steepled his hands and leant forward. 'I'm sorry to say Rudi has met with an accident.'

'What happened?'

'Do you recall his passion for motorbikes?'

'I do.'

'It was dark. He was in Dalan Street, riding home from work. A cart got in his way. There were no witnesses, but people nearby heard a crash and came out of their shops and houses to see what had happened. The motorbike must have skidded when he took avoiding action. It had run into a wall, trapping him underneath. He was lucky the petrol tank didn't explode.'

'Is he badly hurt?'

'Some broken bones, but what concerned the doctors far more was the fact that he lost consciousness for many hours. They feared he might die. Thankfully, it was not the case, but he is still very weak.'

De Silva felt his nails bite into his palms. Quite apart from the fact that he liked Chockalingham, this news spelt potential disaster for his plan. He had been relying on Rudi to take him to see Jayakody. His mind raced. And what was he going to say if Fonseka asked what his business with Rudi was?

'But surely a few broken bones won't hold him back

for long?' he asked, forestalling the question while he cast about for inspiration.

'The situation is more complicated than that. Although he regained consciousness, he remembers nothing. The doctors say they have seen the condition before after a severe trauma. They are unable to say how long the malady will last. Possibly his condition will be permanent.'

With a feeling of deepest dismay, de Silva assimilated the news. This affected far more than their business together. Rudi's whole life was in danger of being ruined. And he'd said he was marrying soon. What of his intended bride? A tragedy for her too.

'Where is he now?'

'At the main hospital. He is being well cared for.'

De Silva took a deep breath and exhaled it slowly. 'I'm very sorry to hear this. I'll visit him before I leave for Nuala.'

'I'm afraid he won't have any idea who you are.'

'All the same I'd like to see him.' He stood up. 'I'm sorry we've met under such sad circumstances, Inspector Fonseka. I'm sure you have work to do, so I won't take up any more of your time.'

Fonseka leant forward and lowered his voice. 'No need to hurry away, Inspector. I may be able to help. Over the last few years, Chockalingham and I have worked closely on numerous cases. Before the accident, he confided in me. I know the reason for your visit.'

De Silva felt a stab of alarm. Rudi hadn't admitted to this. What else had he been hiding?

Fonseka smiled. 'I see you are concerned, Inspector de Silva, but you need not be. The information went no further. And, as matters have turned out, isn't it as well Rudi didn't keep your business to himself?'

De Silva had to admit Fonseka had a point. He only hoped he was as discreet as he professed to be.

'The only thing Rudi didn't mention was the name of

the man you were going to see.'

'Professor Mahindra Jayakody.'

'Had you agreed a time?'

'Rudi mentioned going this afternoon.'

'Right; leave it with me. Where are you staying?'

'The Galle Face Hotel.'

'An excellent choice. I'll telephone you there later once I've spoken to Professor Jayakody.'

Fonseka paused a moment. 'By the way, when I said Rudi confided in me, he didn't tell me exactly why you wanted a second opinion, only that it was in connection with a crime. Are you able to give me any more information?'

'I'd prefer not, sir. If it's all the same to you.'

Fonseka smiled dryly.

'No offence intended,' de Silva added hastily.

'None taken.' Fonseka stood up. 'I look forward to speaking with you later, Inspector.'

* * *

'What a dreadful thing to happen,' said Jane. 'When do you want to go to the hospital?'

'In the morning. From what Fonseka said, I doubt it will make any difference to Rudi when I visit, and I don't want to spoil your day. I promised you lunch and a walk.'

'Oh, you mustn't worry about that.'

'I'm not, I just don't think we need to rush there. I'd like to see Rudi, but tomorrow will do.'

She looked at him shrewdly. 'Do you believe Fonseka?'

'His account of the accident, do you mean?'

'That and about your friend Rudi confiding in him.'

De Silva weighed up the possibilities. 'Yes, I do,' he said at last. 'He told me the street where it happened. It's easy enough to verify the circumstances. And as I know Rudi let slip to Jayakody that another expert had already given an opinion when I expressly asked him to keep it to himself, I'm not all that surprised he spoke to Fonseka.'

He gave a sad smile. 'In the circumstances, I haven't the heart to be angry with him.'

They ate lunch in the hotel's grand dining room where tables laid with silver cutlery and cut glassware were dotted among tall palms in copper pots. They were late and there were few other diners. 'I feel as if I should whisper,' murmured Jane.

De Silva grinned. 'It is rather like being in church. Perhaps it will be more lively tonight.' He poked his fork into the food on his plate. 'But the food is excellent. I was afraid there would be only British dishes on the menu.'

'I expect the chefs in a hotel like this know how to cook both kinds of food well.'

After lunch, they took the promised stroll by the ocean. 'Imagine,' said Jane dreamily. 'If you sailed away, the next time you saw land it would be the Horn of Africa, more than two thousand miles away, but it's less than three hundred miles from one end of Ceylon to the other.'

He raised an eyebrow. 'Is that another hint you'd like to see more of the world?'

'I suppose it is,' she said with a laugh, then sighed. 'I expect it would be very expensive.'

He tucked her hand through his arm. 'We'll manage it somehow, I promise.'

They reached the end of the promenade and turned back towards the hotel. 'Is there something else you'd like to do this afternoon?' she asked.

'I'd like to check out Fonseka's story about the accident.'

'No stone unturned?'

'You know me.'

At the hotel, they hired a rickshaw and told the driver to take them to Dalan Street. 'Wait for us here,' de Silva said, climbing down before helping Jane.

A man standing in the shade of a shop doorway regarded them curiously. A trestle table to his left displayed a pile of mangoes and some bunches of green bananas.

De Silva went over to him. 'Is this your shop?'

The man nodded.

'Have you seen an accident recently? A man falling off a motorbike who was badly injured.'

Other men and a few women and children appeared, all talking at once.

De Silva raised a hand. 'Just one of you tell me.' He pointed to the first man he'd spoken with. 'You'll do.'

'We heard a big noise. Everyone came running out to see what had happened. The motorbike was red.' The man drew a big circle with his hands. 'The elephant of motorbikes.'

That sounded like Rudi.

'It lay on the ground.' He pointed to a shattered wooden cart and a pile of rubble that looked like it had once been a wall. 'Stones were on top of it. The rider was underneath it all. His face and clothes white like a spirit.'

Spare me the flowery language, thought de Silva. 'What did he look like?'

The man studied de Silva impudently. 'Younger than you, sahib. Long legs. Black hair that curled.'

Rudi, undoubtedly.

'Who took him away?'

The man shrugged. 'An ambulance came. I don't know who sent for it.'

'Well, that bears Fonseka's story out,' said de Silva as the rickshaw man took them back to the hotel. He yawned. 'I hope he hasn't telephoned while we were out.'

'I'm sure one of the receptionists will take a message.'

* * *

There were no messages, so they ordered tea in the lounge, but de Silva was unable to settle.

'Do try not to fret, dear,' said Jane. 'I'm sure there's a good reason why he hasn't telephoned yet.'

'I hope this Professor Jayakody hasn't changed his mind. I can't be sure that Fonseka's as persuasive as Rudi.'

'I'm afraid he's all we've got to rely on now.'

She held out a plate of little iced cakes. 'Have one of these. They're delicious.'

De Silva took one and bit into it. She was right: it was good. There was a distinct flavour of cardamom and ginger. He licked a stray dab of icing from a finger and chose another; this time the taste was of rosewater. He was eating the last morsel when a waiter approached. 'There is a call for you, sir,' he said deferentially.

'Thank you, I'll come.'

The telephone rang in the booth in the lobby and he picked up the receiver.

'Inspector de Silva?'

'Speaking; good afternoon, Inspector Fonseka.'

'Professor Jayakody is still able to meet you, but something has come up that makes today difficult. He sends his apologies and suggests you meet tomorrow. Rather than risk causing comment by seeing you in the museum, I'll put my house at your disposal in the evening. You'll be able to speak in private with no fear of anyone asking unwelcome questions.'

'That's very good of you. How do I find your house?'

'I'll send one of my servants to drive you there. Shall we say six o'clock?'

Shame for his lack of trust pricked de Silva. He thanked Fonseka and went back to find Jane.

'It's all arranged.'

'What did I say? There was no need to worry.'

CHAPTER 21

The following morning, they went to the hospital to visit Rudi Chockalingham. The injured policeman was a sorry sight, badly bruised with one arm in plaster from the shoulder to the fingers, and a high collar around his neck that forced his head into an unnaturally stiff, upright position. He studied de Silva's face intently, clearly struggling to remember who he was, but recognition didn't dawn.

'It's best if you don't stay long,' whispered the nurse who bustled into the room carrying a tray on which there was a glass of something unappetising. Despite the cold that still partially clogged de Silva's sensitive nose, he was aware of an evil smell.

'Time for your medicine, Mr Chockalingham,' she said brightly.

A startled expression came into her patient's eyes. With his good hand, he reached for the edge of the sheet and pulled it up to his chin, as if trying to make a barrier. Gently but firmly, the nurse unclasped his fingers and smoothed the sheet down again. She put the glass to his lips; he swallowed then grimaced.

'There,' she chirped. 'I'll bring your lunch in a little while.'

She gave Jane and de Silva a meaningful look. With an awkward smile, de Silva bent down and squeezed Chockalingham's uninjured shoulder. 'We must be going. Get well soon, my friend.'

He straightened up, noting sadly that the blank expression didn't change. But a tear welled up in Chockalingham's eye and slid down his cheek.

* * *

At five minutes to six, de Silva stationed himself in the lobby. He didn't have to wait long before Fonseka's driver came up to him.

'Inspector de Silva?'

'Yes.'

'Please come this way, sahib. The car is outside.'

It was a cream Riley, almost new. Fonseka must be doing well. They cruised through the busy streets, eventually drawing up in front of a pleasant, largish villa in a residential street shaded by jacaranda trees. Fonseka was waiting to greet de Silva and showed him into the drawing room. The man who was already there stood up and held out his hand.

'How do you do, Inspector? I'm Mahindra Jayakody.'

They shook hands and Fonseka gestured to the table by the window. De Silva noticed it was a fine piece of furniture. In fact, the whole room was tastefully furnished with things that must have cost a good deal of money. It would be interesting to know how Fonseka managed it on an inspector's salary.

'Would you like to lay the artefacts you've brought with you out on that table, Inspector?' asked Fonseka.

Opening his bag, de Silva unrolled the cloth he had wrapped the finds in and put them on the table. Jayakody rubbed his hands. 'Let's see what we have here.'

He took an eyeglass out of his pocket and, picking up one of the coins, inspected it slowly. The process continued until he had examined every item.

'Where was all this found?' he asked, putting the last piece down.

De Silva explained, omitting to mention that there had been a dead body close by.

'As you tell me they were found in the Hill Country in the Nuala area, I'm going to hazard a guess that the other man who's given you an opinion on them is Henry Coryat.' He threw a sideways glance in de Silva's direction. 'Am I right?'

There seemed to be no point denying it. De Silva nodded.

'It was a simple enough deduction. I recall that he moved there when he retired from the museum. Coryat never liked city life. Happiest in his own company. Has he found himself somewhere suitably far from human companionship?'

'I think you would say so.'

'I always thought he made the leopard seem gregarious. However, I never faulted him on archaeological matters. I had tremendous respect for him in the professional sphere, so I would be loath to disagree with him. Fortunately, there's no need for conflict here. The coins may be worth a little, but otherwise...'

He shrugged. 'I'm afraid there's nothing that would interest the museum. In the past, some of the inhabitants of Ceylon who were escaping invasion by the kings of southern India, the Portuguese or the Dutch are known to have fled to the hills. They took with them any treasures they could carry, but what you've shown me doesn't qualify. What you've stumbled on is a motley collection, even the best of it not worth much. The kind of thing that's sold in the market to gullible tourists. Have I told you what you wanted to hear, Inspector?' He peered at de Silva. 'I fear not.'

* * *

'I'm sorry you've been disappointed, Inspector,' said Fonseka after Jayakody had gone.

De Silva was still a little wary of giving too much away. 'I wouldn't put it quite like that. Let's say that today has made the situation clearer.'

'Good, that's something to be grateful for. I won't ask you to explain what you mean by it.'

He went over to the sideboard and picked up a bottle. 'Will you have an arrack with me before you go?'

De Silva ought to be getting back to the hotel, but didn't want to appear uncompanionable. 'That would be most welcome.'

Fonseka poured two generous glasses and handed one to de Silva.

'An excellent one,' said de Silva after he had taken the first sip. 'And once again, thank you for helping me out. I'm sorry to have disturbed your evening.'

'It was nothing. My wife's away visiting her family in Jaffna, so I'm glad of some company. The house seems too large if one's alone.'

'Have you lived here long?'

'Since my wife and I married.'

'It's a fine house.'

Fonseka gave him a dry smile. 'I imagine you may have wondered how someone in my position affords it.'

'My dear sir—'

'No need to be embarrassed, it's a reasonable point. We both know that an inspector's salary isn't a princely one. I was fortunate enough to marry a woman who comes from a well-off family. My prospects in the force were adequate to persuade her father that I was an acceptable match.' He chuckled. 'Now I just have to live up to them.'

From the photographs in Fonseka's office, it didn't look as if that was too much of a problem.

They finished the arrack and de Silva accepted a second

glass. After an hour of comparing notes about work and asking after old colleagues, he was driven back to the Galle Face. The rain had started again, veiling the buildings and streets with grey curtains. Pedestrians hunched under their umbrellas, and car wheels kicked up spray.

Jane was reading in the lounge.

'I'm sorry it took so long.'

'Never mind. It's been far too wet to go out and I've been very comfortable. Now, what did Professor Jayakody say?'

'He wasn't impressed with what I showed him. He pretty much confirmed what Coryat said. None of the things are valuable.'

'Oh dear, were you very disappointed?'

He shrugged. 'I didn't want Fonseka to know I was.'

'Why not?'

He tilted his head and sighed. 'Professional pride, I suppose. It makes me look a fool if I give the impression I've pinned all my hopes on one line of inquiry.'

'You're being far too sensitive. Lots of people must have found themselves in that position.'

'Yes, but they might have had a better idea than I do about how they were going to get out of it.'

* * *

Sluicing rain continued for the rest of the evening and was still falling when they retired to their room. In the night, a thunderclap woke de Silva.

As a boy, he'd loved watching tropical storms sweep over the ocean. Sliding his feet into his slippers, he went to the doors to the balcony and quietly opened them. Another clap of thunder boomed, then phosphorescent blue lightning zigzagged down the sky and stabbed into the waves, highlighting the white curls of foam on the dark surface. Exhilarated, he leant on the balcony rail and watched.

'How exciting.' Jane had woken too and come to join him.

'As long as one doesn't have to be out in it.'

She shuddered. 'I hope no fishing boats have sailed.'

'I doubt it. Fishermen usually know when a storm's coming. I'm not sure how. My mother always said that when the frogs croaked more loudly than usual, you could be sure of rain. Her other theory was that when ants built their nests with steeper sides, rain was coming.'

Jane laughed. 'I don't think we need ants and frogs to predict the weather in the monsoon season.' She pulled her shawl round her. 'I'm a bit chilly; I think I'll go back to bed. It's still the middle of the night.'

'I'll come in a minute.'

'You will be careful to fasten the door properly, won't you? The wind's getting up.'

'I will.'

Alone on the balcony, he gazed into the darkness, counting the seconds between the thunderclaps and the lightning. The storm was gradually moving further out into the ocean. What was that expression the British had about inspiration coming in a flash of lightning? He wished it would apply now. Going over everything that had happened since Velu's body had been found, he searched for connections. Clues, anomalies, inconsistencies: anything at all that would provide the key to the puzzle.

Then just as he was ready to give up, the germ of an idea planted itself in his mind. Maybe he didn't need to give up hope after all.

CHAPTER 22

When he went onto the balcony in the morning, he saw a small army of gardeners clearing up the damage the storm had done in the night. Debris littered the lawns, forgotten loungers had been tossed about like rags, and a palm tree lay uprooted on the ground.

'Is there anything you'd like to do now we have the time to ourselves?' asked Jane.

'What would you like to do?'

She put down her coffee cup. 'It would be nice to visit the church I belonged to when I lived here. Apart from that, I'm happy with whatever you want.'

De Silva wasn't sure what that was. The idea that had come to him in the storm was still buzzing about in his head: not quite convincing but refusing to go away entirely. But it was going to be a delicate matter reporting to Archie Clutterbuck that this visit to Colombo had produced nothing. Presenting him with the hunch that had come to him in last night's flash of inspiration – a hunch that hadn't the tiniest shred of evidence to back it up – was unlikely to improve matters.

'Shanti?'

He jerked back to the present.

'Do be honest. Would you rather go home today? I'm sure we could change our tickets if there's room on the sleeper.'

'But I promised you a holiday.'

'I'm happy to go home. According to the forecast in the lobby, there'll be more rain today and it will go on all week. We could go to the museum, but it might be rubbing salt in the wound.'

'That's very considerate of you, my love.'

'I visited it enough times when I lived here. Let's ask reception if they'll call to change our tickets.'

* * *

'One good thing has come out of our journey,' said Jane.

'What's that?'

'Your cold seems to have completely gone.'

He'd forgotten all about it, so she must be right.

'Shall we eat early all the same?' she went on. 'I prefer it when the dining car's quiet.'

'Fine.'

Several Ceylonese dishes were on the menu as well as British food. Glad to see it, de Silva enjoyed his meal then they went back to their compartment to read for a while. De Silva had finished *King Solomon's Mines* before he left Nuala and forgotten to bring a new book, so he settled down with the copy of *The Colombo Times* he'd bought on the station. Skimming the headlines, something about Hatton caught his eye. He turned to the inside page referred to and found the article.

'It sounds like they've got their work cut out down at Hatton,' he remarked to Jane.

She looked up from her book 'Oh?'

'A double murder.'

'Could there be a connection to our murder?'

'It seems unlikely as it's only just happened. In any case, I can do without having to solve any more murders.

It says here there are dozens of people who need to be interviewed.'

'Poor Inspector Singh. I think he likes a quiet life.'

'I sympathise, but we can't always have what we want. I suppose I'd better telephone him in a day or two and ask if he needs my help, unless he calls me first.'

The rest of the evening and the night passed uneventfully, but they arrived late into Kandy due to a fallen tree on the line. They hurried off the train, not wanting to miss the connection to Nanu Oya.

'Oh dear!' exclaimed Jane as they reached the end of the platform. 'In the rush, I think I left my reading spectacles in the compartment. Shanti, would you mind? I think they'll be on the shelf by the window.'

He walked briskly back to the carriage where their compartment had been and swung himself up into the train. The spectacles were where Jane had said they would be. As he snatched them up, a ray of the morning sun came through the window and caught the wire frame. There was a flash of gold. Again, in his mind's eye, de Silva saw that monkey in the tree, playing with something that flashed in the sunlight in the very same way.

When he'd woken up that morning, he'd dismissed the idea that had come to him when he watched the lightning flash the previous night. There wasn't enough to go on, particularly if the good name of one of the British community was at stake. But now the thought returned with greater force. When he'd visited Coryat, the archaeologist had been complaining about his glasses. He'd said he was using old ones because his new ones were lost. What if he'd lost them in the jungle? What if the monkey had been playing with a broken piece of them? Could it be that his hunch wasn't foolish after all?

He jumped down onto the platform and ran to catch up with Jane. 'Your glasses,' he puffed. 'Where did you buy them?'

'The pharmacy. There's nowhere else in Nuala.' She looked puzzled. 'Is it important?'

'It might be. Come on, I'll tell you on the way.'

* * *

'Now, tell me what's so interesting about my glasses,' said Jane as the hill train pulled out of the station. 'They're just ordinary reading glasses that hundreds of people have. I don't think the pharmacy keeps any other kind.'

'That's the point. Do you remember we saw that monkey playing with something that glinted in the sun when we were at the building we found in the jungle?'

She laughed. 'Monkeys don't wear glasses.'

'But they might steal them. Henry Coryat told me he'd lost a pair of glasses.'

'You think he might have lost them in the jungle?'

'Is it too far-fetched? And if he did, it might mean he's involved in this business somehow. Why would he be out there in the middle of nowhere otherwise? When I took the artefacts to show him, maybe he was covering something up.'

'But Professor Jayakody confirmed his opinion. Doesn't that prove Coryat didn't lie to you about their value?'

'Jayakody backed Coryat's opinion on the items I took to Colombo, but what if Coryat's hiding other things? Things found in the jungle that really are valuable?'

'If you're right, he might know who murdered Velu.'

'Exactly.'

'What are you going to do?'

'Speak to Archie Clutterbuck when we get back. I want to have a look round Coryat's house without him there. I need Archie to agree, and to help me with getting Coryat out of the way for a few hours.'

Jane gave him a wry smile. 'You haven't always been too bothered about Archie's permission.'

He grinned. 'That was when I wasn't so sure he'd see things my way.'

CHAPTER 23

'Welcome back,' said Archie Clutterbuck as de Silva was shown into the study at the Residence. 'I'm sorry your holiday was cut short. I take it that something important has come up.'

'I believe it has, sir.'

'Sit yourself down and fire away.'

While de Silva recounted what had gone on in Colombo, Clutterbuck listened in silence, his elbow on the arm of the red-leather armchair, his chin resting on one brawny hand.

De Silva paused before he reached the incident of the flashing spectacles on the Colombo-Kandy sleeper. Doubts entered his mind. Sitting here in Clutterbuck's very masculine study, a potent reminder that the British way was to value facts and figures over intuition, he was suddenly afraid that Clutterbuck would be unimpressed by the moment of revelation. He cast about for more concrete evidence, found none and his confidence deserted him.

Clutterbuck too didn't speak for a few moments. It was a bright morning outside, a welcome change from rain. A shaft of sunlight penetrating the study showed up a light fuzz on Clutterbuck's cheek. De Silva speculated whether a laxer regime of personal grooming than was customary had slipped in while Florence was away. Alternatively, his boss had decided to grow a beard, a brave, one might say foolhardy, choice without his wife's sanction.

'You said something important has come up, de Silva,' he said finally. 'Are you going to tell me what it is? So far, I'm in the dark.'

De Silva took a deep breath. 'It's only a hunch, sir, I can't dignify it with the word proof, but…' He explained about the spectacles and the monkey.

Clutterbuck rubbed his chin; there was a faint rasping sound. 'When my wife tells me the plots of those detective novels she likes so much,' he said pensively, 'I've noticed it's often when the detective observes a tiny detail that he solves the crime. You may have something here. Now, what are we going to do about it?'

De Silva's spirits rose.

'I want a good look round Coryat's house to see if I can find anything to back up my theory.'

'That means you'll need him out of the way. Not easy when he's such a hermit.'

He stood up. 'A whisky and soda usually helps the old creative process. Will you have one?'

'Thank you.'

Ruminatively, they both sat back, glasses in hand. 'No use ringing to say I need him up here on official business,' said Clutterbuck. 'After all the years he's been retired, what official business could there possibly be? It's a pity my wife isn't here; she's so much better that I am at thinking up social occasions. Unfortunately for us, she's currently sailing along the coast of India.'

They lapsed into silence again until there was a knock at the door. Clutterbuck frowned at the interruption. 'Come in.'

A fair, curly head appeared round the door. De Silva recognised Charlie Frobisher.

'Ah, Frobisher. What can I do for you?' Clutterbuck's tone was affable.

'I've a few papers for you to sign, sir, but I'll come back later if it's inconvenient.'

'Leave them with me but stay a moment. You may be able to help us. Fill him in, de Silva.'

When de Silva had finished, the young man frowned. 'It's an interesting theory.' He turned to Clutterbuck. 'Do you think it's worth pursuing, sir?'

'I do. Any ideas how we might get Coryat away from the house, so de Silva can have a good scout round?'

'There's a lunch at the Archaeological Society early next week. It's a special occasion as the current president's retiring.'

'Hmm, so it is,' said Clutterbuck. 'I'd forgotten it was coming up. I believe I'm expected to attend.'

'Do you mean try and get Coryat along to it?' asked de Silva.

'Yes.'

'He's bound to wonder why he's been asked so late; or at all,' said Clutterbuck gloomily.

'They must have known each other pretty well in the past,' Frobisher went on. 'There was a time when Coryat was very active in Ceylon's archaeological affairs. We'd have to cook up a story about a lost invitation to explain away why he's been asked so late, but that's not impossible.' He grinned. 'The committee of the Nuala Archaeological Society has never been renowned for its organisational skills on anything after about 500AD.'

'Good: we have a plan.' Clutterbuck rubbed his hands. 'Put it into action, would you, Frobisher?'

* * *

'You don't need to tell me it went well,' said Jane with a smile. 'I see that from your face.'

'It certainly did, and that young Frobisher came up with a plan that should work.'

He ran through the conversation.

'How marvellous if this turns out to be your break-through.'

'A breakthrough, but who knows to what? The tendrils of this case may stretch a long way. We have Velu's murder; the village headman's grandson missing; Rudi severely injured after what may, or may not, have been an accident, and, on second thoughts, those two murders at Hatton may be connected somehow. The timing's suspicious.'

'Well, let's hope that Coryat's house will provide an answer.'

'If lunch is nearly ready, I'll eat here. After that, I'd better go down to the police station. See what Prasanna and Nadar have been up to in my absence.'

* * *

The weather seemed bent on reinforcing Jane's optimistic mood. The sunny morning had turned into a glorious afternoon. Only a few gauzy clouds, that reminded de Silva of fish scales, interrupted the blue of the sky. The colours in the bazaar looked so much more vivid than they did when it was raining; there were smiles on people's faces.

He pulled up in front of the police station and went in. The public room was empty. For a moment, he wondered if Prasanna and Nadar had been called down to Hatton to help with the double murder investigation, but if they had, why hadn't they locked up?

There was a more likely explanation. He padded past the public desk and out to the backyard beyond the kitchen area. Sure enough, Nadar was defending a makeshift wicket and Prasanna bowling.

'I hoped to find you working on police business, not practising your cricket.'

The two young men flushed. 'Only in our lunch hour, sir,' Prasanna said apologetically.

De Silva looked at his watch. 'Well, I want to see you at work in fifteen minutes. Has there been any news from Hatton?'

'About the murders? No, sir.'

'Right.'

He debated whether to tell them what had transpired in Colombo then decided against it. Time enough to fill them in when he'd paid his visit to Coryat's house. It wasn't that he didn't trust Prasanna and Nadar, but the fewer people who knew about the plan the better. 'Carry on, gentlemen.'

In his office, he opened the few letters on his desk. None of them were urgent. He swung his chair round and gazed out of the window. It was going to be hard to wait until the day of this lunch. He wondered if he ought to telephone Inspector Singh at Hatton to see if he needed a hand, then decided against it. When he got the call from Clutterbuck, it would be inconvenient being down at Hatton. He would also have to explain away why he suddenly needed to desert the investigation. Best to hold back for the moment. If Singh called, he'd have to make some excuse or send Prasanna or Nadar down.

The telephone rang, and he lifted the receiver. 'It's Mr Clutterbuck for you, sir,' said Nadar.

'Put him through.'

'De Silva? Frobisher's laid the bait. Cross your fingers Coryat takes it.'

CHAPTER 24

He set off just before dawn on the day of the Archaeological Society's lunch. In the darkness, the road to Coryat's house was hair-raising. One wrong move and the Morris would be over the precipice and into the abyss. Mud, washed down by weeks of monsoon rain, slicked the surface, making it even more treacherous. It seemed like an eternity passed by the time the ground levelled out and the road continued over the forested plateau he remembered from the last time.

He relaxed his grip on the steering wheel. He had estimated that Coryat wouldn't need to leave for Nuala until around ten. A glance at the clock on the dashboard told him he still had about two hours to get into position and see the archaeologist go. He would turn off the Morris's headlights for the last bit of the journey to make his presence less obvious. Thankfully, there had been no rain since he set out from Sunnybank – the journey had been quite alarming enough without it – but now the darkness was receding, he saw that the sky was peppered with ominous clouds. More rain wouldn't be long coming.

A mile or so from the bungalow, he pulled over and parked the Morris out of sight of the road. Shrugging on his raincoat, he started to walk. Eventually, the bungalow loomed ahead, looking even more desolate in the poor light than the first time he'd seen it. Cautiously, he worked his way round, staying in the shelter of the trees that bordered the garden, until he had a good view of the driveway. Once he left the belt of trees, he would have very little cover, just a few bushes to hide behind. He thought of Coryat's servants; he'd have to take his chance that they were less than vigilant.

He glanced at his watch: not quite a quarter to ten. Thunder rumbled in the distance. If Coryat left it to the last moment, he was going to get very wet waiting for him.

A fat drop of water, then another and another set the leaves around him quivering. Soon, the rain sluiced down, plastering his hair to his hatless head. There had better be something worth finding in Coryat's place. At least he should have plenty of time to make a thorough search. Apparently, what with the post-prandial toasts and speeches, the lunch would last for at least four hours.

A door banged, and he snapped to attention. With a raincoat draped over his head, Coryat emerged from the bungalow. He hurried over to the elderly Austin parked to one side of the drive, opened the driver's door and got in. A few moments later, the car moved off, kicking up water from its tyres.

De Silva waited until the Austin was out of sight before leaving the shelter of the trees. Knuckling the rain out of his eyes, he jogged across the ill-kempt lawn, ducking behind the bushes as he reached them; waiting a few moments in case he heard voices, but all that disturbed the silence was the sound of birds singing. Either the servants weren't about, or they were sleeping.

Coryat would probably have locked the front door, so he had better start at the back. He patted the pocket where he had secreted a small lock-picking kit in case he needed it. He hoped, however, that he wouldn't. He was out of practice with breaking and entering.

To his relief, on the second attempt, he found a door that

was unlocked. As he pushed it open, the hinges creaked in protest. He looked down at his feet and noticed that the soles of his shoes were muddy. He wiped them carefully on the frayed doormat then stepped inside. Pausing, he listened intently for several moments then, emboldened by the silence, went on.

Beyond the small lobby, the panelled room he entered was the study he remembered from his previous visit. The curtains were pulled halfway across the window and he didn't dare turn on the light. Still unaccustomed to the semi-darkness, he stumbled against a pile of boxes that had been left on the floor. Hastily, he bent down to steady them and saw that they contained stones of different shapes and sizes, some of them with inscriptions in an alphabet he didn't recognise.

A search of the desk drawers revealed piles of paper covered in spidery handwriting, presumably Coryat's. There was nothing de Silva wouldn't have expected: descriptions of artefacts, notes on their condition and provenance. Most of the objects catalogued appeared to have come from the great archaeological sites at Anuradhapura and Polonnaruwa. From the faded state of the ink, he guessed that the work had been done many years ago. There were also old letters addressed to Coryat from universities and institutions in England and Ceylon asking his advice on various matters.

He worked methodically through the rest of the room, opening cupboards and drawers, some empty and some crammed with files and papers. The man certainly had a fine collection of books; the aroma of leather and old paper was enticing. In other circumstances, de Silva would have enjoyed spending a few hours browsing the shelves. He debated whether he should pull a few out to check them, but when he ran his finger along the tops of the spines, the dust that came away convinced him it wouldn't be necessary.

Finally, he used the torch from Coryat's desk to shine a light up the chimney and make sure there was nothing hidden in its dark recess. As he straightened up, he noticed a khaki canvas bag propped against the wall. Inside was an ancient rifle. From the amount of tarnish on the metal fittings, it looked as if it hadn't been used for years. Unlike Archie Clutterbuck's study, there were no trophies or photographs of fishing or shooting successes on display. Presumably, Coryat wasn't a sportsman. He probably kept the rifle for protection, although it was hard to see who he would need protection from in this God-forsaken spot.

Satisfied there was nothing more to examine, he went out to the hall. The bungalow wasn't extensive; the rooms he hadn't yet seen comprised a drawing room, a dining room, two bedrooms, and a very old-fashioned bathroom. As he'd been led to believe on his first visit, the cooking must all be done in the separate building where he'd met Coryat's servant.

De Silva's hopes of finding something useful dwindled as he continued his search. Was he wrong about Coryat? Perhaps he had been too quick to jump to the conclusion that the monkey in the jungle had been playing with broken spectacles. Coryat seemed negligent about his living conditions. Maybe he took the same attitude to the rest of his life. He could have lost his glasses anywhere and simply not got round to replacing them.

He looked out of the window in the dining room, the last room left to search. Rain was falling heavily, leeching the little remaining colour from the forlorn garden. The idea of looking round the outside of the house was distinctly unappealing, but he ought to do so. There might be a cellar reached from the garden, or outbuildings where something was hidden.

He decided to leave through the back lobby where he had come in. He paused on the threshold to the study, his sensitive nose picking up a smell he hadn't noticed before: the scent of rain and damp grass. Was one of Coryat's servants snooping around after all, or had he simply failed to close the outer door properly when he came in? That was careless. He'd better check if rain had driven in and, if necessary, clean up the floor to cover his traces.

He listened, but all he heard was rain hammering on the roof and the wind rattling the windows. His imagination was playing tricks; he was alone in the house, and it was time he left. But two steps into the study, he noticed something had changed since he arrived.

He froze. The khaki canvas bag no longer stood upright against the wall. Instead, it was lying in a crumpled heap on the floor. There was no sign of the rifle. He heard a movement behind him and swung round.

Coryat stood a few feet away, his eyes in line with the rifle's sights. 'I considered putting a bullet in your back, Inspector, but my respect for the law convinced me to give you the opportunity of explaining yourself. But first, please take off your raincoat and jacket. I assume you have a gun underneath. Oblige me by removing it and putting it on my desk.'

De Silva hesitated then eased one arm out of the raincoat. He wondered how fast Coryat was on the trigger. Was it feasible to pull out the Webley and shoot him first? He was at least twenty years older than de Silva and his reactions might be slower.

'Back up a few steps,' Coryat said sharply. 'I wouldn't get any ideas if I were you. I'm a better shot than you might think.'

Reluctantly, de Silva complied and put the raincoat down on the floor. His jacket followed.

Coryat smiled grimly at the sight of the Webley.

'I thought as much. Standard colonial issue but effective nonetheless.' He gestured with the rifle, 'Unbuckle the holster and put it down then get your back to the wall.'

De Silva did as he was told, glancing at the desk as he passed it. There were several objects that might do as missiles, but it would be risky. Coryat shook his head. 'I repeat, Inspector, don't get any ideas.

'That's better,' he said as the wall pressed against de Silva's back.

Coryat raised an eyebrow. 'Such a pity I had to disappoint the Archaeological Society. I hope the lunch goes well without me. You see, I never had any intention of attending. I smelt a rat at being given an invitation after so long, and I proved to be right. In any case, you and I will have a much more interesting time. Shall we start with your telling me exactly why you're here?'

'I'd prefer to start by reminding you that obstructing a policeman in the performance of his duties carries a severe penalty, Mr Coryat.'

'Oh, I have no intention of obstructing you, Inspector. You're clearly an optimist. No, I intend to kill you. But first, I'd be interested in knowing exactly what you've found out. Fonseka told me about your visit to Colombo, and I doubt you made the perilous journey to my little lair purely for social reasons.'

There was an icy gleam in Coryat's eyes. De Silva felt his heartbeat quicken. So Fonseka was in league with Coryat. He should never have trusted the chief inspector. Were they behind Rudi's accident too? 'You won't get away with it,' he said, in the calmest tone he was capable of. 'People know I was coming here.'

'Ah, but they'll have no proof that you arrived, will they? I'm still a highly respected man in my field, Inspector. Plenty of people will bear witness to my character. I'll say that you never got here. Unsurprising really, in view of the state of the road. I had to abandon my planned journey to Nuala because the conditions were too dangerous for driving.

In a week or two, your car will be discovered burnt out in the jungle below the hillside. I'll spare you the unpleasant experience of a protracted death. You'll know nothing of the car's plunge over the edge. The impact would probably be sufficient to set the vehicle on fire, but a liberal dousing with petrol before the final act should ensure a dramatic denouement.'

De Silva dug his nails into his palms, trying to use the pain to control his rising panic. An innocent man wouldn't threaten to kill him. Coryat must be deep in whatever criminal activity had taken place. The murder was probably just the tip of the iceberg. In some way, he needed to convince Coryat that there was already plenty of evidence stacked against him, and it would be better to come clean now and ask for clemency. He'd have to make assumptions and hope he touched a raw nerve.

'You may be able to silence me, Mr Coryat, but that won't be the end of it. The authorities know you're guilty of murder.'

Coryat frowned. 'I had nothing to do with it. It was their decision. The man was in the wrong place at the wrong time, meddling in things he didn't understand.'

'They?'

A furtive look came over Coryat's face. He'd been caught unawares and said too much. 'I can't tell you that.'

'But you know who killed the villager, Velu.'

Coryat shrugged, regaining his composure. 'Velu? I don't recognise the name.'

'Perhaps you didn't know his name, but you're aware of who I'm talking about. And then there's Inspector Chockalingham. The motorbike crash was no accident, was it?'

If Coryat was rattled he didn't show it. De Silva tried again.

'The people you're dealing with are ruthless. Violence

161

is nothing to them. If you're not afraid, you should be. As soon as you've served your purpose, they'll dispose of you, and they won't be scrupulous about how they do it. Tell me everything, and I can help you. Nothing's worth risking your life for.'

A slow smile crept over Coryat's face. 'Oh, I assure you some things are. I might as well tell you now that the artefacts you brought to show me are worth far more than I led you to believe, but they pale into insignificance compared with the rest of the finds we made in the jungle. The supreme prize, however, outshines them all.'

Keeping hold of the rifle, he moved to one side of the fireplace and pressed gently on a panel. The wood swung out like a small door to reveal a shallow compartment.

Coryat reached in and pulled out a bundle of black cloth. Reverentially, he placed it on the desk then stepped back. He nodded to de Silva. 'Unwrap it if you like; I feel I owe you that. Not many men have the chance to see something as exquisite as this before they die. You should count yourself privileged.'

De Silva took a step forward and Coryat raised the rifle. 'Slowly though. Remember what I said about not getting any ideas.'

More cautiously, de Silva moved to the desk. The bundle was remarkably heavy for its size. Whatever was inside must be made of stone or metal.

As the cloth peeled away, he saw it was a gold statue. About eight inches high, it showed the Buddha in the lotus position, his right hand raised, palm outwards in a gesture of benediction, and his left across his body. The tips of the forefinger and thumb met in a perfect circle. The statue was an object of such beauty that, despite the danger he was in, de Silva was lost in contemplation for a few moments.

'Astonishing, isn't it?' asked Coryat quietly.
'Yes.'

'Five hundred years old; a miracle it's survived in such good condition. I believe it may have been buried for a long time.'

'How did you know where to search?'

Coryat nodded to one of the bookshelves. 'Many of my books are old. I've long been interested in a legend one of them mentions about treasure hidden in the area by fugitives leaving the coastal regions to escape the Portuguese invaders. A combination of educated guesswork and luck showed me the way to it.'

It might be worth trying to play on the man's vanity. Maybe he could be distracted for long enough from his murderous intentions for de Silva to find a chink in his armour.

'It's a remarkable piece. It must be one most archaeologists never dream of finding in their whole career.'

Coryat smiled. 'You flatter me, Inspector, but I'm afraid it won't help your situation. It's a pity in a way. I have nothing against you personally. If you hadn't poked your nose into my business, I wouldn't have to kill you.'

De Silva tried to ignore the chilling threat.

'Did you find other pieces as valuable?'

A scowl replaced Coryat's smile. 'I've wasted enough time. Put your car keys on the desk. I assume you didn't walk here. Tell me where you left it and we'll go.'

Slowly, de Silva fished in his pocket for his keys. Coryat was too far away to throw them at him with sufficient force to disable him temporarily and get control. He pinned his hopes on there being a chance on the way to the car. He would pretend to lose the way to buy time.

Coryat was just picking up his own keys when a doorbell rang. If whoever it was had driven in, the noise of the rain had masked their approach. An irritable expression came over Coryat's face.

'Why are they coming here today?' he muttered.

He jerked his head towards the largest of the cupboards. 'Get in there and don't make any noise. If you try to call for help, you'll regret it more than you can possibly imagine.'

Reluctantly, de Silva did as he was told.

The cupboard was empty apart from an old coat on the hanging rail and a pair of what seemed to be heavy boots. The stuffy air reeked of mouldering wool. He heard the click of the lock turning, followed by receding footsteps. Coryat must be going to answer the door.

De Silva pulled out his handkerchief and held it over his nose and mouth. It was dusty in the cupboard, but he couldn't afford to sneeze or cough. It was obviously going to be unwise to move around either if the mysterious visitor, or visitors, came into the study.

Voices and footsteps grew louder. He guessed there were two men, maybe three, with Coryat. The one who was talking spoke English with a strong accent. De Silva frowned. Wasn't it familiar?

When Coryat answered, he talked fast, as if he was nervous. De Silva struggled to make out what he and the man were saying but only managed to catch something about an agreement to hand over money. Coryat's agitation was even more apparent as the conversation went on. There were other noises. It sounded like the room was being searched.

De Silva only just stopped himself from recoiling when the door of the cupboard in which he was imprisoned shook.

'It's locked, boss,' said a rough voice, very close to his ear. His stomach churned. Any minute now, Coryat would have to open the door. From what he'd said earlier, thought de Silva, after that, it will all be over for me.

'Open it,' the man with the accent barked. His name suddenly came to de Silva. It was Joseph Edelman.

'There's nothing that would interest you,' Coryat said sharply.

De Silva heard the sneer in Edelman's voice. 'Then why lock it?'

'My servant. He's untrustworthy. I keep important academic papers there that I don't want him meddling with.'

Edelman laughed. 'An illiterate peasant? Do you really expect me to believe he'd be interested in your tedious outpourings, or have the faintest idea how to find anyone who'd give him a handful of rupees for them? Open it!'

'I don't remember where I put the key.'

'Then break it open.'

'Okay, boss.'

The voice was a new one. Edelman must have two men with him.

A heavy blow shook the cupboard door, swiftly followed by a second and a third. De Silva wondered which of the men would kill him, not that it really mattered. He just hoped they carried out their task quickly.

His breath caught in his throat, and the roar of blood filled his ears. He watched the slit of light around the door as it widened. Then suddenly, the blows stopped. There was a thud, as if a body had fallen to the floor, and a long, low groan of pain that sent a shiver down de Silva's spine.

'Ah, I see you decided to keep this intriguing statue for yourself.'

The voice was Edelman's, oily with sarcasm. 'You should have asked me, my friend.'

'Take it! And take back the money.'

Coryat spoke so fast that his words tumbled over each other. 'It's in my safe. Take it, it's yours. I don't want anything more to do with this.'

'It's a pity you didn't come to that conclusion earlier.'

De Silva heard a blow and a muffled scream.

'Get him out of here,' Edelman said coldly. 'One of you can finish him off outside.'

De Silva heard sounds of a struggle; they must be dragging Coryat away. There was nothing he could do to help him. He'd be lucky to save his own skin. How much time did he have before the men came back? Presumably, they'd want to finish the search.

He waited until the sounds died away then, with a gasp of relief, allowed himself to move and clear his throat. He studied the door in the dim light. Edelman's gorilla had succeeded in making some impression on it. What a pity his lock-picking kit was still in his jacket though.

He slid to the floor and put his feet flat against the wood, pushing as hard as he could, despite the twinge from his still-weak ankle. The door didn't budge. No escape that way after all. He scrambled up awkwardly and winced. He'd put his hand on one of the boots. There was something sharp there. He picked it up and explored it with his fingers. His luck hadn't entirely deserted him: the sole was heavily studded.

Pulling off his shoes, he tugged on the boots then slid down to the floor again. After a few minutes of kicking at the area of the lock, he took off one boot and hauled himself to his feet. Using the studded sole like a can opener, he worked away at the gap, stopping every few minutes to listen for sounds of the men returning.

At last the lock gave way. He was free, but what now?

CHAPTER 25

There was no sign of his uniform jacket or the Webley in the study. Coryat must have had time to hide them before he went to let Edelman and his thugs in. It was too risky to spend time looking, but his raincoat was over the back of a chair. He donned it and turned up the collar then grabbed his car keys before stepping out into the rain.

At the front door, he waited a moment to check there was no one to see him then set off. He was almost across the drive, heading for the trees to work his way back to the car when he heard a shout. His heart hammering, he realised he'd been spotted. He sprinted the rest of the way into the trees. When he reached them, he leant against the trunk of a coconut palm to catch his breath. He wasn't as fit as he had been in his Colombo days. Luck needed to be on his side if he was to outwit Edelman and his thugs.

He thought quickly. The route he had taken on the way in had been near to the edge of the tree cover. It would be better to go deeper, where it was easier to conceal oneself. Already, his pursuers were likely to be close behind him. His only comfort was that the rain was slackening. The moisture it had created was evaporating in the heat, wreathing everything in a misty vapour that might give him an advantage.

Waterlogged soil squelched beneath his feet as he pressed on, scrambling over fallen trees and edging through undergrowth. Behind him, curses and the crack of breaking branches told him that his pursuers hadn't given up. The noise grew louder as the minutes ticked by. His heart pounded against his ribs. To be caught meant certain death.

A few more yards and a new terror gripped him. The jungle was always a confusing place, even when you weren't being chased by murderous thugs. In his agitation, he hadn't been going in the direction of the car; he was at the edge of the plateau where Coryat's house stood.

His feet shot away, and he only saved himself from falling further by grabbing one of the thick lianas snaking down from a nearby tree. The rough bark scraped his palms. He stifled a cry of pain as his arms were almost wrenched from their sockets. Bile surged into his mouth. He'd already lost a considerable amount of height, but ahead the ground fell away in an even more abrupt descent to the floor of the jungle. Stars exploded in front of his eyes as he clung to the liana, blinking frantically. He had to control himself. If he panicked, there was no hope.

Peering down, he saw that fifty or so feet below him there was a flattish ledge, probably made by a landslide. It was impossible to see how far it extended around the flank of the hill, but it looked to project out at least fifteen feet into the void. If he reached it, it would give him a place to rest and gather his wits. It might also provide a route towards a gentler slope he could climb to regain the plateau.

The descent to the ledge was, however, a perilous one. His hands burned from clutching at lianas and bushes to slow his progress. Sometimes he clung like a limpet, letting himself down as gently as possible by using tree roots as a crude stairway. His palms sweated as he fumbled for handholds on the slimy wood. With every slip and slither, the sickness of fear increased, threatening to overwhelm him.

A crow landed on a branch above a fallen tree trunk where he had briefly stopped to rest. It fixed him with a mocking eye. It was all very well for the wretched bird. It could fly.

The need to concentrate on every move had so consumed him that he had almost forgotten about his pursuers, but a shout from above brought back the full force of the danger he was in. The shout was followed by an eerie scream.

A figure fell down the almost sheer face of the plateau, tossed and buffeted as it glanced off the jungle's unforgiving vegetation. It looked like a ragdoll, but de Silva realised it was a man. His fall was broken by the ledge. There he came to rest, sprawled across a rotting tree trunk, his head thrown back as if he was gazing up at the sky. There was no movement. De Silva didn't recognise him. He must be one of Edelman's thugs who had lost his footing in the chase.

Voices were still shouting. Edelman and his remaining henchman? What if they tried to climb down? They might not risk it, but he was probably within range of their guns. He edged closer to the tree trunk and wormed his way into the gap between it and the ground. As the voices rose and fell, he closed his eyes and waited for what seemed like an eternity. At last silence descended.

Wriggling out from under the trunk, he slid the rest of the way down to the ledge. The man was indeed dead. A trail of blood leaked from one side of his mouth. From the way his head lolled, de Silva guessed that his neck was broken. He was taller than de Silva, and far more powerfully built. De Silva was glad he hadn't had to face him in a fight. Now that he posed no threat, he felt a twinge of pity for him. All violent ends were difficult to witness.

He crouched beside the dead man and closed his sightless eyes. There was nothing he could do but leave him to the jungle. It would deal with him in its own way.

Now he was alone, he was aware of it returning to its secret life. Mostly unseen, or seen only in flashes of vivid colour, birds hooted and whistled. Leaves rustled and small creatures going about their business disturbed the undergrowth. He hoped there were no snakes nearby. Well, if there were, there was nothing for it now but to carry on along the ledge and hope it would eventually bring him to safety.

It was slow going scrambling over loose rocks and fallen trees. He wiped the grime from the dial of his watch and checked the time. Nearly half past three. In less than three hours, the sun would go down; the last thing he wanted was to be marooned on this hillside at night. So far, he had encountered nothing more dangerous than a few monkeys who had skittered off at his approach, but far more alarming creatures might emerge to hunt after sunset.

The ledge had become a rocky cleft in the plateau's wall. Soon, it cut such a steep diagonal that his arms ached from hauling himself up it. Then he felt a jolt of fear. Beyond an outcrop of rock, his path vanished into thin air.

Horror overwhelmed him. Even if he had the strength to go back to the ledge where Edelman's thug lay dead, he faced a very long climb and, possibly, Edelman and the other man. But the climb ahead of him was no more inviting and to miss his footing would mean certain death.

He had to decide quickly. Every minute he delayed, his knees felt weaker. In a few moments, the temptation to give up, step over the side of the cliff and be done with it would be irresistible. He rubbed his sweating palms on the back of his trousers and reached for the first handhold.

Gradually, he fell into a rhythm: move one hand, move one foot; creep slowly upwards, one step at a time. Sometimes a rock gave way, or a liana wasn't strong enough to hold his weight, and he lost height, but he surprised himself by how calmly he managed to focus on the task in hand. He wondered whether he might even find that he had conquered his fear of heights.

But the top was still fifty feet away when his newly

found confidence evaporated like early morning mist. A tree root that had seemed solid enough to take his weight snapped. In the nick of time, he grabbed another root and it held, but then he was stuck. The old paralysis seeped over him. The drop beckoned.

The sun had started to sink behind the tree line. A distant rumble of thunder warned of rain. Soon it pattered on the leaves around him. If it was heavy, and it was likely to be, it would be impossible for him to climb any higher. Even if he found handholds, they would be too wet to grip.

It was over.

He turned his head and saw the sky was streaked with crimson. Light-headed with hunger and thirst, a profound weariness swept over him. If only he could tell Jane one last time that he loved her.

Then from above, a voice called his name. He glimpsed a halo of golden curls. There was a cry, and wings buffeted his face. Out of the dusk, a figure descended towards him, bathed in light. Was it one of those angels the congregation sang about in Jane's church on Sundays? Was he saved?

His body sagged as strong arms enfolded him. He closed his eyes and let himself be borne aloft.

CHAPTER 26

'De Silva! Wake up, man!'

With a struggle, de Silva opened his eyes to see Archie Clutterbuck standing over him, hurricane lamp in hand and rain streaming off his coat and hat. Beyond him, more hurricane lamps illuminated the concerned faces of Prasanna and Nadar. In their glistening, dark raingear, they looked uncannily like a pair of crows.

'That's better.' Archie turned to Prasanna and Nadar. 'Don't just stand there! Help him up.'

Prasanna hurried forward and, with his and Nadar's help, de Silva struggled to his feet.

A face framed by yellow, curly hair, swam into view. No angel: it was attached to the body of Charlie Frobisher.

'I'm sorry about the cuts and bruises, Inspector. It wasn't as easy to pull you up as I'd hoped, and when I disturbed that bird from its roost, I thought I wasn't even going to be able to hold onto you.'

'It was you,' de Silva said wonderingly.

Frobisher looked puzzled as he untied the rope that had been anchoring him to a nearby tree from round his waist. 'Why yes, sir.'

'I don't know how to—'

'Never mind, never mind,' intervened Clutterbuck. 'Plenty of time for thanks when we've got you dry and warm. You're not in good shape. We came out as soon as we realised something might be wrong. Coryat not turning up at the Residence rang the alarm bells. I wish we'd found you sooner, but this place is damned difficult to search. Lucky there are several of us, and that we came in the Hillman because of the bad road. The kit we took into the jungle was still in the boot, and Frobisher had the foresight to bring the rope along. Without it, both of you would probably have been lost over the edge.'

'Coryat's been murdered—'

De Silva wanted to continue, but he was too exhausted. He felt the weight of a thick blanket being draped round his shoulders.

'We know,' said Clutterbuck. 'We've already been up to the house. His body was in the garden. We found another man dead on the hillside. But you can tell us everything when we've got you to shelter. The rain's coming again. Where's the Morris by the way? You're in no fit state to be at the wheel. Frobisher can drive her up for you.'

Teeth chattering, de Silva handed over the keys − miraculously still in his trouser pocket − and explained as best he could where the Morris would be found.

'Off you go, Frobisher,' said Clutterbuck. 'We'll carry the inspector to the house and meet you there.'

* * *

By the time they reached the house, the Morris was already parked on the drive next to the Hillman. Charlie Frobisher came forward to greet them.

'Help us get de Silva inside,' said Clutterbuck. 'There must be some brandy around. I think we could all do with a tot.'

De Silva felt powerless to argue as he was helped into Coryat's study. Frobisher left him with Nadar and went to find where Coryat kept his brandy. When he returned a few minutes later, he put a glass to de Silva's lips. He drank and immediately started to cough.

'Steady, old chap.' Clutterbuck had just come back into the room. 'Now, are you up to telling us what happened here?'

De Silva struggled to stop spluttering. His whole body ached.

'Take your time.'

Archie Clutterbuck listened attentively as de Silva recounted the afternoon's events, only interrupting to ask who Joseph Edelman was. De Silva realised he'd never mentioned the incident on the train when he made his report. He'd been bound up in his theories about Coryat. Quickly, he explained.

'So, Coryat tried to hide the statue from this man Edelman,' said Clutterbuck. 'I imagine we're too late to recover it. Edelman's probably taken it with him. I wonder how he found out Coryat tried to cheat him.'

He turned to Charlie Frobisher. 'It's worth doing a thorough search in case Coryat had anything else tucked away. Prasanna and Nadar can stay and help you. Oh, and find somewhere safe to put those bodies until the undertakers can pick them up. Whatever they did, I don't want them torn to pieces by some animal. I'll drive de Silva back to Nuala. I think he's done enough for one night.'

* * *

'Thank goodness that nice young man Charlie Frobisher's good at climbing,' said Jane when Clutterbuck had gone.

De Silva sat on the edge of the bathtub while she sponged his cuts and grazes and applied ointment and plasters. He had resisted her suggestion that they call Doctor

Hebden out. He still ached, but, thankfully, his wounds were superficial.

'According to Archie, he's very keen and hopes to spend his next long leave in the Himalayas.'

'How exciting.'

She stood up. 'There; all done. We'll have some supper then I want you to rest. It's a good thing Archie said he doesn't want to hear you've gone back to work for a couple of days. We've had quite enough excitement for the time being. No more adventures, please. What if you'd ended up dead like Coryat?'

'What indeed. But I don't know about resting. There's still a lot to be done. There's no sign of Edelman. Archie's going to alert the Colombo force and have a watch put on the ports, but there's far more to this than finding Edelman, and it's a delicate matter. Now we know Fonseka's involved and probably Professor Jayakody too, we don't want either of them tipped off until the picture's clear.'

He fell silent, and Jane looked at him quizzically. 'You should be proud of the part you've played, dear. Without you, Coryat might never have been exposed. But I can tell something's troubling you.'

'I still don't know what Velu's part in all this was, or why he was killed. And then there's poor Rudi. Quite apart from the fact that I'd like to see him fit and well again, I could do with having any relevant information that's locked away in that brain of his.'

'And I'm sure you will, given time.'

'I just hope it won't be too late.'

Jane patted his hand. 'I think you're bothered that the Colombo force will be taking over.'

De Silva shrugged. 'Not really… well, maybe I am. But Archie's in possession of all the facts now, and he's right when he says my presence in Colombo might arouse suspicion. Much better to leave it to the Colombo boys on the ground and just go back to being a provincial policeman.'

'And a very good one,' said Jane firmly.

'Thank you for the vote of confidence, my love.'

CHAPTER 27

The next day, de Silva passed a restful morning, even taking a stroll in the garden when it wasn't raining. By lunchtime, however, enforced idleness left him feeling like an elephant with a sore head. When the telephone rang in the hall as they were finishing their meal, he hurried out to see who was calling.

'It is Sahib Clutterbuck for you, sahib.' The servant held out the receiver and de Silva seized it.

Clutterbuck's tone was business-like. 'Everything's under control, de Silva. The Colombo force is swinging into action, and we have the watches set on the ports.'

'That's good to hear, sir. Have they any information about the statue?'

'The one Coryat was so excited about? No, it's still missing. I don't want to ask too many questions at the museum right now. I plan to wait until it turns up and then decide what to do about ascertaining its value.'

There was a pause. 'Well, I'll leave you to get on with whatever you were doing when I called. Nothing too energetic I trust. Don't forget my advice.'

'Thank you, sir.'

De Silva put the receiver down and rolled his eyes. Advice? It had practically been an order. He sighed. Under normal circumstances he would enjoy time off for reading and chatting to Jane, but it was unbearable to have the case taken out of his hands before he'd solved it.

He went back to the drawing room and sat down.

Jane smiled. 'Is that good news from Archie, dear?'

'Oh, absolutely. He's made all the arrangements as we discussed.'

'Good.'

She glanced out of the window at the steadily falling rain. 'I expect this will go on until dinner time at least. What a pity. Still, I have a good book to be getting on with – *Death in Mesopotamia*, Mrs Christie's latest. Why don't you read too? It's far too wet to be out in the garden.'

'Yes, you're right. Just the afternoon for a good book.'

He went to the bookshelf and chose something by Dickens he hadn't read before then settled in his armchair. But the story didn't hold his attention for long. Soon his thoughts turned back to Coryat. He hated loose ends and it was even worse when no one would give him the chance to tie them up. He worried that if Edelman and the stolen statue were found, there would be very little enthusiasm left for hunting down Velu's killer. What about Rudi too? If the crash hadn't been an accident, was the perpetrator going to escape punishment for his crime?

CHAPTER 28

By Saturday, de Silva had finished the Dickens, played several games of Scrabble with Jane, and studied his garden catalogues, choosing some new varieties of potatoes for the gardener to plant if the rain ever stopped. He liked the sound of a new variety called Arran Pilot and a long, knobbly one with the strange name Pink Fir Apple, that looked more like a pink ginger root.

He and Jane had also driven down to Hatton for her to collect a dress she'd had made at a shop she favoured there. He'd debated dropping in at the police station to see how Inspector Singh was getting on with his murder investigation, it was still in his mind that there might be a connection, but Jane's pursed lips indicated it wasn't advisable.

'The police in Colombo are perfectly capable of looking into that if need be,' she said firmly.

'I've left Prasanna and Nadar on their own long enough,' he said after breakfast.

'They promised to telephone if something came up they couldn't deal with. And life in Nuala's rarely as dramatic as it has been recently.'

'I know, but I don't want them to think I've forgotten them.'

'I'm sure they won't.' She raised an eyebrow. 'And think of the advantages for our cricket team.'

'That's what's bothering me. I think I'll just go down for a few hours. Make sure they're keeping their socks up. This life of leisure can't go on indefinitely.'

When he reached the station, Prasanna and Nadar were in the public room, giving every indication of being hard at work. He wondered whether Jane had telephoned after he left Sunnybank to ensure he was given the impression everything was under control. He wouldn't put it past her.

'Have you had any news about Mr Coryat's murder, sir?' asked Prasanna after they'd exchanged greetings.

'No,' de Silva said flatly. The young men's surprised expressions made him regret he'd answered so baldly. 'Of course, I'm being kept up to date with the case,' he added hastily.

He picked up the file in front of Prasanna. It was labelled "Traffic Offences".

'I'll look over this in my office. Bring my tea in, would you?'

When he'd closed his office door, he dumped the file on the desk. It landed with a thunk, raising a puff of dust. A case that might be of national importance was unfolding in Colombo and here he was, reduced to checking routine paperwork.

He sat down and opened the file. Scanning the first page, he jabbed a comment into the margin and made a hole in the paper. The ink smudged. As he reached for a piece of blotting paper, his arm caught the inkwell and it nearly fell on the floor; he caught it just in time. At the same moment, the telephone rang. He put the inkwell back in its place and picked up the receiver.

'There's a call from Colombo, sir,' said Nadar.

De Silva's pulse quickened.

'From police headquarters? Do they give a name?'

'No name, sir, and it's not from headquarters.'

He frowned. 'Where then?'

'The General Post Office.'

An irritable expression came over de Silva's face. Who on earth would be calling him from the General Post Office? Was he going to be put in charge of missing parcels and letters now?

He exhaled wearily. 'You'd better put them through.'

'Is that Inspector Shanti de Silva?' asked a tremulous voice. It was a woman's.

'Yes; to who am I speaking?'

'My name is Ayomi.'

The name meant nothing to him. 'What can I do for you, Ayomi?'

There was a long pause. De Silva wondered what it could be that was so difficult to say. At last the woman spoke again.

'I am engaged to be married to Rudi Chockalingham.'

Ah, this was interesting. 'Go on.'

'He desperately wants to speak with you, Inspector de Silva. He...' There was another pause.

'Can he come to the telephone?'

'No, he's not here. He's still in the hospital. The doctors won't let him out until they think he is well, and his memory has come back.'

'You say he desperately wants to speak to me, but how does he remember who I am?'

'Some of his memory has come back, but he has only told me that.'

'That's good news. But why has he only told you?'

'Because he doesn't remember everything. He knows you came to see him, but not the reason for it. People come from the police headquarters asking him questions, but they won't tell him what it's all about. He's afraid he's made mistakes and is in trouble. Please, Inspector, help us.'

De Silva sucked air through his teeth, considering. 'It will take me a good while to come down to Colombo. Is there any way Rudi and I can talk on the telephone?'

'No, sir. He's not allowed any calls.'

'Very well, I'll come down as soon as I can, but it's a considerable journey. I won't be with you before Monday. Where will I find you?'

'Oh, thank you, thank you! I work at the Post Office. I finish at five o'clock.'

'Until five o'clock on Monday then.'

He ended the call and leant back in his chair; the traffic file forgotten. What would be revealed on Monday, and why was Rudi unwilling to talk to anyone but him? The thought crossed his mind that Rudi remembered perfectly well what had happened before his accident and what his mistakes had been. What he didn't know was quite how much hot water he was in, or how best to get out of it.

It was good to be back in the game. But for the moment, apart from telling Jane, he'd keep this development to himself.

CHAPTER 29

On arrival in Colombo, he booked into a hotel and dropped off his bag. Given the time of his meeting with Ayomi, it would be too late to return to Nuala that night. He bought breakfast at a street stall then wondered what to do until it was time to meet Ayomi.

On his principle of no stone unturned, it occurred to him that it would be a good idea to visit the museum. He might be able to find out more about Professor Jayakody. If the museum was like most public institutions, it would have photographs of its officers and reams of information about them on display. It was a habit he'd always resisted at the police station in Nuala. He knew what he looked like, and he spent enough time putting up with the sight of Prasanna's and Nadar's ugly mugs.

He took the precaution of buying a length of cloth in the market and went back to the hotel. Fashioning a turban that covered a large part of his face, he put on the traditional tunic and trousers he had brought with him to go to the hospital then looked in the mirror. Good: if he saw Jayakody at the museum, he doubted the man would recognise him.

At the museum, he found what he was looking for in the entrance hall. A series of wooden boards were attached to one of the walls, displaying the names, photographs and academic qualifications of the museum's officials.

It took him some time to find Mahindra Jayakody, largely because he didn't recognise the man's photograph. Jayakody's domed head betrayed no hint of hair. He stared solemnly out at the viewer through horn-rimmed spectacles; his light-brown skin was pock-marked and his nose bulbous. In short, he wasn't the man de Silva had met at Fonseka's house.

* * *

Workers streamed out of the General Post Office shortly after five o'clock. De Silva had been waiting outside for several minutes, admiring the magnificence of the place. Its rusticated stone walls, pedimented windows and massive columns reminded him of the Italian Renaissance palaces he'd seen photographs of in one of Jane's art books. Strange that in all his years in Colombo, he'd never looked at it properly before.

He wondered how he would find Ayomi among all these people, but it was she who found him. She was older than he'd expected and far less glamorous than Rudi's previous girlfriends. She had a lovely smile, and dark eyes that looked as if they didn't miss much.

'It was clever of you to guess who I was,' said de Silva after the initial pleasantries were over. 'I thought it was advisable not to come in uniform if I'm to get in to see Rudi without any questions being asked.'

She smiled. 'Rudi described you very well.'

'Did he now? What did he tell you?'

'He said you had kind eyes.'

'Hmm.'

He swiftly warmed to Rudi's betrothed as they made the journey to the hospital and joined the crowd waiting for visiting time to commence. They had agreed that de Silva would claim to be Rudi's cousin if anyone asked.

'Do you think anyone will stop us?' he asked.

'Sometimes there's a guard at the door, but not always. It's not allowed, but they go out to smoke.'

De Silva had spent many hours thinking about how he would handle the business. He always concluded that it was impossible to believe Rudi had acted dishonestly. Whatever he'd done, de Silva would hear his confession in confidence. If that was the wrong thing to do, and he couldn't persuade Rudi to give himself up, he'd take the consequences.

Fortunately, there was no guard at Rudi's door. A look of immense relief flooded his face when they walked in the room. He hauled himself up on his pillows. 'Shanti! You've come! I'm so grateful.'

He and Ayomi exchanged a kiss then she sat down on a chair in the corner to listen.

Starting at the beginning, de Silva told the story of the villager, Velu's murder; the finds in the jungle; his encounter with Joseph Edelman on the train; the meeting with Fonseka and the man who had turned out to be impersonating Jayakody; Henry Coryat's murder, and the missing statue.

'It's my belief your crash was no accident,' he concluded. 'I think Fonseka arranged it. He wanted you out of the way.'

Rudi ran a hand through his hair and scowled. 'I should never have talked to Fonseka.'

'Did you tell him I was coming to Colombo and the reason for the visit?'

Rudi flushed. 'I told him enough, I'm afraid. Fonseka! Of all people. How could I have been such a fool? He's fiercely ambitious. Always wants to know everything that's going on.' He laughed bitterly. 'Usually with a view to stabbing a colleague in the back so he can take another step up over their body. I've always been wary around him. I think he knows I don't trust him.'

'Yes, but how did the subject come up in the first place?'

'I wrote down your name and number while we were on the telephone and left the note on my desk. I was called away and it was only when I got back that I realised it was on view. Fonseka must have seen it, and the Nuala telephone number made him suspicious. He stopped me in the corridor and said he'd intended for weeks to buy me a drink to celebrate my engagement. I accepted, and it went from there.'

He smiled ruefully. 'He bought the best arrack. You know how it is.'

De Silva refrained from saying that drinking too much was a mistake he'd avoided in over twenty years of police work. His friend had suffered enough for his lapse of caution.

'What a mess. And it's all because of me.'

'Stop blaming yourself; there'll be a way out.'

'I hope so,' Rudi said with a groan. 'What will you do now?'

'Fonseka took your place by underhand means, and he cancelled Jayakody and got me to see an impostor. He's involved with Edelman. Let's hope no one else at the station is, but we can't be too careful. I want to talk to Archie Clutterbuck, the assistant government agent in Nuala, before going any further. I'll advise we wait until Edelman's found before we pick up Fonseka.'

'What do you want me to do?'

'Stay right where you are and keep up your story that you can't remember anything. I'll insist the guard on your room is tightened up too. The last thing we want is Fonseka trying to silence you.'

A movement in the corner reminded him that Ayomi was still there.

'I'm sorry,' he said. 'I didn't mean to frighten you.'

'It's alright, Inspector. It's no surprise Rudi's in danger. But I'll sleep more easily now we have you to help us.'

* * *

Rudi was lucky to have found Ayomi, reflected de Silva as he left the hospital. With her beside him, he might make old bones.

But the current danger to his old friend mustn't be underestimated. The sooner he got back to Nuala and reported to Archie Clutterbuck, the better. It would be a relief when Edelman was tracked down. He wondered if Fonseka would lose his nerve and try to escape with him.

He ate at the same street stall where he had bought breakfast. They cooked an excellent curry. He washed the meal down with coconut water and went to a bar for a glass of arrack before going back to his hotel.

He telephoned Jane from there to tell her he would be home the following day. Briefly, he filled her in on events in Colombo.

'Your poor friend, Rudi,' she said. 'I hope he won't be in trouble. Can Archie be persuaded to intercede on his behalf?'

'I'll do my best. I'll have to stay here tonight and let you know in the morning when my train will get back to Nanu Oya.'

'Sleep well, dear.'

'You too.'

CHAPTER 30

'I told you to take it easy for a few days,' Archie Clutterbuck said severely. His expression softened. 'But I suppose the result justifies the disregard for my orders.'

'Thank you, sir.'

'I'll have a word with the Chief of Police in Colombo. If there are no other blemishes on your friend's record, I expect his lapse will be overlooked.'

'There won't be. I'm sure of it.'

'Good. I agree it's best to wait until Edelman's found before arresting Fonseka. That's a job for the Colombo force. If they catch Edelman with his loot he may confess. Otherwise, you'll need to go down to give evidence. Are you prepared to testify you're certain that the man you heard at Coryat's house was Edelman?'

'I am, sir.'

'As there were no witnesses, I have my doubts we'll be able to prove your theory about Rudi Chockalingham's accident, but we've enough on Fonseka otherwise.' He scratched his chin. 'I wonder who impersonated Jayakody. It would be interesting to find out. Fonseka will have to be convinced it's worth his while to divulge the man's name. I suppose none of the other faces on the boards at the museum rang a bell?'

'No, sir.'

'Well, I think that wraps things up for the moment. I'll say it again: take things easy for a few days.'

'What about Velu, sir?'

'Velu?'

'The murdered villager.'

'Ah, him. So much has happened since then, I almost forgot.' He sat silent for a few moments, hands clasped and thumbs slowly rolling round each other. 'Are you certain there's a connection?' he asked eventually.

'The finds near his body, and the timing, so close to Coryat's murder, convince me of it.'

Clutterbuck shrugged. 'Very well; you'd better pursue that line of inquiry.'

Walking back to the Morris, de Silva's step was lighter than it had been on arrival at the Residence. He had considerable cause for satisfaction. But he would have felt even better if Clutterbuck's reaction to the mention of Velu had been less grudging. The man hadn't been the most upstanding member of society, but he still deserved justice. And, de Silva vowed, although at present it's not entirely clear how, I'm going to see that he gets it.

* * *

'Good news,' he said when he got home.

'I'm so glad, dear. Tell me all about it.'

'I think Rudi's in the clear. Archie's on our side. The Colombo boys are still looking for Edelman though.'

'Will you be needed again?'

'Only if Edelman refuses to confess once he's arrested. If that's the case, although I can't swear to it he killed Coryat personally, I can testify that he ordered him to be killed. It should be enough to put him away for a few years.'

'Well, you can relax now.'

'I plan to, and I promise to forget about work for the moment. What about going out tonight? Would you like to see a film?'

'Lovely. They're showing a Charlie Chaplin this week.'
'Then let's go.'

* * *

De Silva was surprised to see Sergeant Prasanna and his wife Kuveni leaving the cinema after the film. He thought they preferred Indian films with their lavish costumes and singing and dancing.

'I wanted to see the famous Mr Chaplin,' Kuveni said when Jane and de Silva caught up with them.

'I hope you enjoyed the film,' said Jane.

'We laughed, but it was also sad.'

'Yes, when you stop to think about it, *Modern Times* is sad as well as funny. Two sides of the same coin.'

'I may not be in until Monday, Prasanna,' said de Silva. 'I'll bring you and Nadar up to date then. Have you anything to report in the meantime?'

'No, sir. It's been quiet.'

'Good. Enjoy the rest of your evening.'

* * *

Inspector Singh's call interrupted the quiet Monday morning.

'How's the investigation going?' asked de Silva. 'Do you need my help?'

'It's good of you to offer, but that's all settled. It was a domestic affair. The man had decided to do away with his wife and mother-in-law.'

'Nasty.'

'Yes.'

'We must meet for a drink sometime. Compare notes.'

'An excellent idea. Maybe sooner than you think. I

promised to let you know if that village headman's grandson turned up. One of my men caught him stealing in the bazaar a few days ago. I'm holding him until the magistrate sits later this week.'

De Silva felt a jolt of excitement. This was better luck than he'd anticipated. 'I'll come this afternoon if it's alright with you.'

'Of course; I look forward to it.'

* * *

The grandson eyed de Silva and Singh warily when they walked into the interview room. He was girlishly handsome with black hair that curled to his shoulders. The whisper of a moustache darkened his upper lip.

'This is Inspector de Silva of the Nuala Police,' said Singh. 'He has some questions. It will go better for you if you answer them truthfully.'

The young man's expression was sulky, but de Silva saw there was also fear. He decided to start with a kindly approach that was probably far gentler than the treatment the lad's grandfather would have meted out to him.

Reluctantly at first, but becoming more forthcoming with de Silva's judicious prompting, the grandson admitted he had been present when Velu was murdered.

'Who were you working for?' asked de Silva.

The young man shivered and cast a longing glance at the barred window where a meagre ray of sunshine struggled to penetrate the shadowy room. 'I never knew their names.'

'Were they white men?'

'Yes.'

'Describe them to me.'

When he finished, de Silva nodded. 'It sounds like Edelman and Coryat.'

'I'll check if Coryat's body's still at the undertakers,' said Singh. 'If so, the lad can identify it.'

A queasy look clouded the young man's face. Not a hardened villain then, thought de Silva.

'What were you doing for them?'

'Digging. They were looking for treasure. After all the rain, it was dangerous. We'd already had one mudslide, but they wouldn't let us stop.' Sweat beaded his brow. 'I wanted to get away. I wouldn't have been there at all if it hadn't been for Velu. He owed money. The moneylender was going to have him beaten up if he didn't pay.'

'What about you? Did you owe money as well?'

The young man's gaze shifted away. 'No,' he muttered.

'Perhaps you wanted to make a quick buck?'

There was no answer, and de Silva didn't press him.

'Who killed Velu?'

'The fat man.'

'How did he sound?'

'He spoke English, but he didn't sound like a Britisher.'

Edelman: de Silva was certain of it.

'Why did he kill Velu?'

'Velu was crazy. He argued about how much he was being paid. He said it wasn't enough, and he wouldn't go on. The fat man said he had to finish the job. Velu said no. The fat man raised his gun.' He mimicked the action. 'And *pouf...*'

'What happened after that?'

'I ran. They weren't fast enough to catch me. It was getting dark, and I lost them in the jungle. I stayed there for a long time.'

'What did you live on?'

The young man pulled a face. 'Grubs, lizards. Sometimes birds.'

'I imagine such a life doesn't appeal for long.'

The young man shrugged.

A thought came to de Silva. 'You said the work was dangerous because of the rain. Was it raining when Velu was shot?'

The question seemed to surprise the young man. 'It was in the morning, but it stopped.'

De Silva nodded. 'Thank you, you've been a help. I'm sure Inspector Singh here will see to it that the magistrate's made aware of that.'

Singh went to the door and called a constable. 'We're done. Take him back to his cell.'

So, de Silva reflected, as the young man was led away, Jane had been right. The scream he'd heard on that rainy evening on the old Hatton Road had been the wind playing a trick on his ears. But how lucky he had doubted her. If it hadn't been for that, he and Prasanna and Nadar wouldn't have gone back to search, and Velu's body would probably never have been found.

CHAPTER 31

A few weeks later

The great and the good of Colombo were gathered in the museum to celebrate the arrival of a new item for the collection: the statue recovered from Joseph Edelman along with the rest of the loot he had planned to smuggle to Europe. He had finally been tracked down trying to board a ship at Jaffna. It was likely de Silva would have to testify, but otherwise, all that was left for him to do was identify the man who had impersonated Professor Jayakody. After studying numerous files of photographs held at the Colombo station, he was able to tell them he was a man called Zamir Maheshwari.

Fonseka had also been arrested. He denied having anything to do with Rudi Chockalingham's accident. Hoping for lenience, he had turned King's evidence against Edelman, but his career in the police was over.

The gold statue took pride of place in a large display cabinet in the centre of the great hall, surrounded by the best of the other finds.

'I feel out of place,' de Silva said to Jane as they stood together nearby.

'What nonsense! If it wasn't for you, the case would never have been solved.'

'A few other people helped.'

'Your contribution was the most important.'

She sipped her champagne and looked round the hall. 'The Governor General and his wife are here. Look, they're talking to the Petries. Archie's with them too, and Florence, back from her holiday. We should go and say hello.'

De Silva hesitated. His work had brought him into contact with the Petries several times and he liked them, but the Governor General and his lady were a more daunting prospect.

Jane wasn't to be resisted, however, and they joined the group.

William Petrie made the introductions. Afterwards, de Silva couldn't remember what the Governor General had said, but he was aware it was very complimentary. William congratulated him, and Lady Caroline gave him one of her sweet smiles. 'Another victory for you, Inspector,' she said. 'Success is becoming a habit.'

De Silva feared he might flush like a schoolboy. He was saved by the Director of the Museum who came to claim the attention of the Governor General and his wife and the Petries. Florence started to engage Jane in a long conversation about her travels. De Silva found himself alone with Archie.

'Excellent outcome, eh, de Silva?' he remarked. He stared down into his champagne glass. 'Do you like this stuff? Overrated to my way of thinking. Give me a decent whisky any day.'

'I agree with you there.'

Clutterbuck gestured to the statue. 'Pretty piece, isn't it? I'm told it's worth a king's ransom. Good to know it's staying here where it belongs, not being spirited back to London.'

'Two things still puzzle me, sir.'

'Mm?'

'Firstly, how did Joseph Edelman know that Henry Coryat was hiding something from him?'

'I'm sorry, I thought you'd been told. Fonseka revealed it

was thanks to the man you identified as Zamir Maheshwari. He may be a crook, but he knows his onions.'

What on earth did onions have to do with it, wondered de Silva.

'Edelman's a canny customer. He decided he wanted another opinion apart from Coryat's. Edelman knows about jewellery, but he's not an expert on antiquities. Maybe he's been cheated before. Maheshwari already knew quite a lot about the hoard from old tales in the antiquities' world. Apparently, there are theories going back many years that it was hidden somewhere in the Hill Country. He was suspicious about Coryat's assertion he'd handed over everything, especially as, in his view, Coryat had exaggerated the value of some pieces.'

'Why would he do that?'

'Edelman was paying him for his work. I imagine Coryat thought Edelman would be more generous if he believed Coryat had found him a fortune. When Fonseka tipped Edelman off that you were coming to Colombo, they thought you might have some good pieces. Hence the episode on the train.'

'That's the other thing I don't understand. How did Edelman know who I was? It can't just have been inspired guesswork, especially as he would have been looking for a man on his own and not a couple.'

'It wasn't. Fonseka purloined the photo from your old file at Colombo headquarters and sent it to him.'

'So, Edelman set up the robbery?'

'Indeed. The unfortunate thief was his servant. It's not clear yet whether Edelman always intended to do away with him, or whether that was unplanned.'

De Silva thought back to the moment on the train when the thief had fallen out of the door. In the confusion of the robbery, de Silva hadn't seen his face very clearly, and it had been too dark to make out what was going on between him and Edelman at the train door. Edelman could easily have pushed him.

He also remembered seeing Edelman leave the station concourse. Why hadn't he noticed at the time? The driver had helped Edelman into the car, not the servant, although he'd been with him at the start of the journey, and Edelman had talked about him being on the train after the staged robbery. No servant would be so disrespectful as to take a seat in a car before his master. Clearly, the reason why the servant hadn't held the door was that he was lying dead by the train track.

'In any case,' Clutterbuck continued, 'Once Edelman heard you had nothing of great value to show, he came straight back to Nuala to confront Henry Coryat.'

'Why would Coryat get involved in the first place? I thought he was highly respected in the academic world. He seemed to live frugally. Surely he wasn't after money?'

'Not money; although we believe the lure of owning a precious object may have swayed him. There was something else though. It was hushed up at the time, but several years ago, Coryat stole from the museum. When he was found out, he returned his loot, and was allowed to retire with his honour intact. He moved to Nuala, presumably hoping to put everything behind him and spend the rest of his life writing up his researches. He would have succeeded if Edelman hadn't heard a rumour about him. He probed further and threatened to expose Coryat if he didn't help him.'

'Why not just use Zamir Maheshwari? Wouldn't it have been less risky?'

'Maheshwari likes to keep in the background. I'm surprised he agreed to meet you at Fonseka's house. Probably Edelman insisted he did, anticipating you wouldn't be parted from your treasures. I'm afraid he's slipped through the net, but one day he'll make a mistake.'

Florence and Jane joined them; Florence radiant from

her cruise. 'My dear Inspector,' she trilled. 'Such a wonderful experience. You and Jane simply must go.'

'I feel as if I already have,' Jane whispered as Archie and Florence moved away to talk to other friends and acquaintances. 'Florence is so full of her tales of the sea.'

Tucking her arm in his, he smiled. 'If you'd like to, we'll find a way.'

He glanced around the hall. 'There's Charlie Frobisher over there. Shall we go and say hello?'

'Do let's. He's such a delightful young man.'

She contemplated Frobisher for a moment. 'Florence tells me that Archie says he has a very promising career ahead of him. Does he have a wife?'

'Not so far as I'm aware.'

'You know how keen the Colonial service is for its staff to be married.'

He looked at her with an expression that pantomimed despair. 'Don't tell me you're plotting already.'

She smiled. 'As if I'd dream of it.'

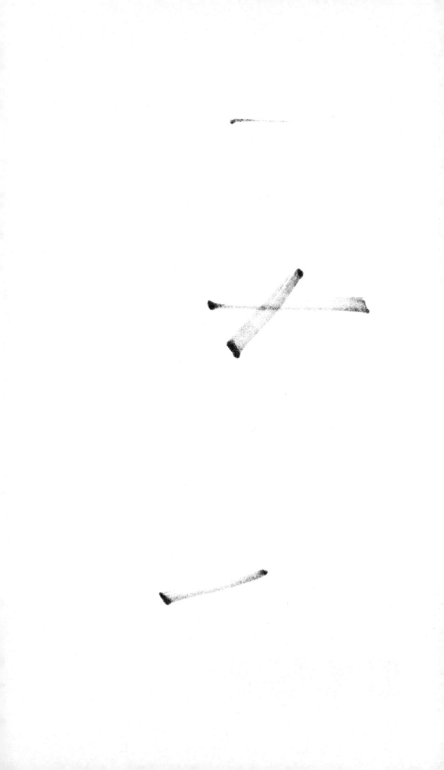

METUCHEN PUBLIC LIBRARY

DISCARD

METUCHEN PUBLIC LIBRARY
METUCHEN, NJ 08840

OCT 3 1 2022

Made in the USA
Coppell, TX
22 November 2020

41887043R00125